ONCE
UPON A TIME

Henry *and* Violet

ONCE
UPON A TIME

Henry _and_ Violet

By **Michelle Zink**

Based on the ABC Television series created by
Edward Kitsis & Adam Horowitz

KINGSWELL TEEN

Los Angeles • New York

Published by Kingswell Teen, an imprint of Disney Book Group. No part
of this book may be reproduced or transmitted in any form or by any
means, electronic or mechanical, including photocopying, recording,
or by any information storage and retrieval system, without written
permission from the publisher.

For information address Kingswell Teen,
1200 Grand Central Avenue, Glendale, California 91201.

Editorial Director: Wendy Lefkon
Executive Editor: Laura Hopper
Cover designed by Julie Rose

ISBN 978-1-368-02370-2
FAC-020093-18082

Printed in the United States of America
First Hardcover Edition, May 2018
10 9 8 7 6 5 4 3 2 1

www.disneybooks.com

Dedicated to everyone
who is ready for a new fairy tale

ONCE UPON A TIME

Henry and Violet

By Michelle Zink

One

The minute she opened her eyes, Violet knew the next two days were going to be special. It was the first day of an overnight field trip to New York City. This wasn't the first time she'd been to the bustling metropolis, but it would be the first time she dared something as bold as sneaking away with Henry. The bus was leaving Storybrooke at five a.m. sharp, and she stretched in bed and allowed herself a few precious moments in the dark to think about him.

It was because of Henry that she'd been living a real-life fairy tale. Because of him that she'd made friends so quickly, that she felt at home against all odds. He was the one who had shown her how to work her cell phone, how to stream movies on her computer, how to dance to modern music.

There was nothing she didn't like about him, from the way his brown hair sometimes flopped over his forehead to the warmth in his eyes when he looked at her to the way he always made her laugh. He was her best friend, the one person besides her father she could count on no matter what.

There was only one problem. Or to be exact, a whole town of them.

Despite the fact that they saw each other nearly every day, it was becoming increasingly difficult to escape the overattentive gaze of the people of Storybrooke, her father being the worst of the culprits.

The next two days would be different.

They would have hours to hold hands and steal kisses without looking over their shoulders. They wouldn't have to worry about Granny reporting back to Emma that they'd been spotted at their favorite make-out spot behind the diner or about Mary Margaret coming upon them snuggling in the halls of Storybrooke High. Emma wouldn't appear with a sudden errand for Henry, and Violet's father wouldn't make that sound he made when dinner was already on the table and Violet was on the phone with Henry.

Finally, they would be able to spend time together without every adult in Storybrooke seeking to put distance between them—her father the most enthusiastically of all.

She tried to ignore the nervousness that fluttered in her stomach when she thought about sneaking away from their classmates on the field trip, not to mention Emma and Killian, who planned to chaperone. It was only for a few hours the first day, and whatever trouble she and Henry got into later would be worth the time spent alone, to say nothing of the other reason for her master plan.

The thought of it prompted her to sit up in bed. She stretched in the darkened room, then reached to turn on the bedside lamp. After tying back her long dark hair with the elastic she kept on her nightstand, she flung her feet over the side of the bed and crossed to the laptop on her desk.

She clicked refresh on the website she'd been monitoring for the past five days and watched as it loaded.

The notebook with the cracked leather cover was still there, and she scrolled down, reading again the description of the journal filled with intricate drawings and familiar handwriting. She could hardly believe it was within reach.

She clicked on the picture of the first page, her eyes moving over her father's signature and the date, left incomplete when he had been transported suddenly and mysteriously to Camelot.

Hank Morgan
1887–

He'd spoken often of the notebook he'd left behind in Connecticut. She'd thought she understood his sadness, but it wasn't until she'd found the notebook online at Back in the Day, an antiques store in New York City, that she truly felt the breadth of all he'd lost.

The pages were filled with drawings of complex inventions, some of which she understood while others remained a mystery. Each illustration was accompanied by detailed notes, and Violet had immediately been able to imagine her father before he'd left Connecticut, head bent as he scribbled furiously in its pages. Even more vividly, she saw him as he'd been the past three years in Storybrooke, his head bent to empty pages as he struggled for new ideas.

It had been easy in Camelot. He had, after all, come from a much more advanced time. All his ideas had seemed like magic to their friends in the kingdom.

But the world had advanced while he'd been gone. He tried to put on a happy face, but she saw the toll it had taken for him to leave everything behind again. The notebook would be just the thing to lift his spirits.

She closed her computer and started getting ready, washing her face and brushing her teeth and adding her toiletries to the overnight bag she'd packed the day before. When she was done, she slipped a floral sundress over her head and slid her feet into flats, then went to work fixing her hair. She did one last check to make sure she had everything—especially the money she would need to make an offer on the notebook—and stepped into the hall.

The house had felt foreign and strange when they'd first moved in, with its smooth walls and the heat that emerged like magic from vents in the ceiling. It had been almost too warm in the winter and she'd spent her first Christmas Eve with her bedroom window open a crack in spite of the frigid temperatures outside.

But over the past three years she'd come to love the soft feel of carpet under her feet in her bedroom, the cool wood floors in the halls. She'd gotten used to being warm when it was cold outside and to the hot baths she could run in an instant in a bathroom that was all hers. They'd had to board Nicodemus at a nearby stable since there wasn't enough room at the house, but it was a small price to pay. She rode him almost every day and she felt comfortable and safe as she descended the stairs amid the smell of frying bacon.

Her father was sliding scrambled eggs onto a plate when she reached the kitchen. He looked up as she entered the room.

"Good morning," he said. "I thought you might need a proper breakfast today."

She smiled and stood on tiptoe to kiss his cheek. He was forever worrying about her lack of interest in breakfast.

"I think you might be right." She would happily eat breakfast if it would prolong his smile, even if the twinkle was still missing from his eyes. "It looks delicious."

"Are you excited for the trip?" he asked, arranging the bacon and a piece of toast around the eggs and setting the plate in front of her.

She picked up her fork. "Very. I love New York."

He nodded a little sadly as he poured her orange juice, and she wished she could stuff the words back in her mouth. They hadn't talked much about what would happen after high school. There was the last month of junior year to get through, then summer before she had to start thinking about senior year and college, but they both knew the moment was coming when she would have to decide what was next.

She'd avoided talking about it with him, had avoided even thinking about it too much. She couldn't imagine leaving her father in Storybrooke when he was still so sad. She remembered the notebook and felt a surge of hope. Maybe it would inspire him to start inventing again and give him something to focus on when she left home.

He set the juice on the table and took the seat next to her. "Emma and Killian are still chaperoning?"

"Yes, and there will be other chaperones, too. Plus, I think Mary Margaret is standing in for Mrs. Holt." Mrs. Holt, everyone's favorite French teacher, had had to leave unexpectedly when her baby arrived a month ahead of her due date. Henry's grandmother Mary Margaret had offered to take the other teacher's place on the trip to New York City. "There's no need to worry."

It wasn't easy having a father who'd left the Land Without Stories in 1889 for the even more conservative court at Camelot. In the years he'd been in the other realm, he'd adopted all of their customs and expectations. It had taken her and Henry nearly six months of surreptitious dating to share a kiss thanks to the impossibility of finding time alone. Her father had been like a guard dog with supernatural hearing and eyes in the back of his head. It had gotten a little better, but he still asked a lot of questions when they spent time together. Chaperones had been at the top of his list when she'd brought home the permission form for the overnight trip to New York.

"Will this be enough for everything you need?" he asked, passing her a folded stack of cash.

"I don't need it," she protested. "I have money."

He always had plenty of business in the carriage house at the back of their property, where he repaired electronics and small machinery, but she tried to pay her own way with earnings from her job at the bookstore whenever possible. It cost a lot of money to live in the modern world, and even though he never complained, she knew it couldn't be easy.

"Nonsense. I'm your father. Take the money."

She knew from the gruffness in his voice there would be no arguing the point. She took the money and squeezed his hand. "Thank you."

Theirs was an unspoken arrangement: she wouldn't get too mushy with him and he would try to listen when she really needed to talk about her feelings, even if he squirmed while she did it. She hoped if she went away to college he would find someone else to fuss over and that whoever it was would understand him and let him be himself.

She nibbled at her toast, her earlier excitement suddenly tempered by the feeling that it couldn't last. That all of them—she and her father and even Henry—were balanced on the knife's edge of change that would come for them whether they were ready or not.

She forced the thought aside and focused on her breakfast, making a point to eat every bite in silent thanks for her father's effort. She was being pulled into the vortex of the melancholy that had been stalking her father. The trip to the city was just the thing to set everything right. She would spend the day holding Henry's hand and kissing him whenever she wanted. She would get the notebook for her father.

Everything would be fine.

Two

Henry Mills could hardly contain his excitement as he packed his backpack. It was more than the trip to New York City; it was the idea of spending so much time with Violet that he was really looking forward to.

They'd gotten pretty good at finding opportunities to sneak away from her father's watchful eyes, but the moments were always stolen, both of them all too aware that an interruption was inevitable. Maybe it would be one of Henry's moms, Emma or Regina, not-so-innocently bringing a fresh bowl of popcorn into the living room when he and Violet were watching a movie. Or it could be his grandfather pretending not to know he was interrupting when he happened upon them kissing behind Granny's Diner. More likely it would be Sir Morgan, who seemed to have a gift for knowing exactly when things were heating up between his daughter and Henry.

He and Violet were usually able to laugh it off, but they were both looking forward to two whole days outside Storybrooke. He wasn't thrilled with the idea of sneaking away from the group—and his parents—on the first day of the field trip, but if getting the notebook that had belonged to Violet's father meant Henry and Violet would have time alone, he was all in.

Sir Morgan had seemed happy to be back when he and Violet first came to live in Storybrooke, but over the past year he'd become more and more withdrawn, saving what little enthusiasm he had for keeping Henry from being alone with Violet. Henry hated seeing the change in the stubborn, vital man who'd returned with them from Camelot, but most of all he hated seeing the sadness in Violet's eyes and knowing there was nothing he could do about it.

It had been easy when she first came to Storybrooke. There had been so much she didn't know: how to stream music and listen to it through headphones, how to buy things and make sure she got the right change, how to use the internet and a cell phone.

Now it was like she'd been there forever, and Henry had to admit he missed knowing she needed him. As if that wasn't enough, there was the prospect of graduation the following year. Henry wished he could be as sure as Violet—who wanted to go to college—about his future, but the truth was, he didn't know what he wanted to do next. He'd been in Storybrooke his whole life, and while college was the most obvious option, he wasn't entirely sure it was for him.

The thought of him and Violet on different tracks was like a distant storm cloud hanging over their relationship. He tried not to dwell on it. Instead, he focused on what he knew—namely, that he loved Violet Morgan. He loved the way her cheeks turned pink when she was happy or excited and the way she bit her lip when she was thinking hard about something. He loved to watch her ride Nicodemus, how beautiful and free she looked when she took the horse through his exercises. He loved the way she talked, kind of fancy like she was still back in Camelot, and the kindness she showed to others. In fact, he couldn't think of a single thing about her he didn't like.

They would find a way to make their future work, whatever it held.

"Henry! Emma's here!"

He zipped up his backpack and grabbed his duffel bag as Regina's voice carried from downstairs. Having two moms was cool most of the time. He had two bedrooms in two houses and moved easily back and forth between them. Killian was there when Henry was on Mom overload, and his grandparents' house was always available as an escape. All in all, his life was pretty awesome, and he had a spring in his step as he headed down the stairs.

"Hey, kid," Emma said when he walked into the living room. "You ready for this?"

In her red jacket and black jeans, she was the opposite

of Regina, who always wore tailored slacks and a blouse. It wasn't the only way they were different. Emma had long blond hair, while Regina had shorter black hair. Emma was funny, while Regina was strict. Between the two of them, they covered all the parental bases. It had taken a long time to get to a place where they were family, but he felt lucky to have them both.

"Ready," he said.

"You haven't eaten breakfast," Regina protested.

"I'm not hungry."

She held out a brown paper bag. "I had a feeling you were going to say that. This should tide you and Violet over until you get to the city."

Henry gave her a hug. "Thanks, Mom."

"You're welcome." Regina looked at Emma. "You going to survive two whole days with those monsters?"

Emma laughed, and Henry cringed when she ruffled his hair like he was still ten years old. "It's been a while since I've been up this early, but it's going to be great. Killian can keep me company while Henry pretends not to know me."

"Better you than me," Regina said. "I'm going back to bed for more beauty sleep."

"Speaking of Killian," Emma said, "we should go. He's probably changing all my radio stations again."

Henry didn't bother reminding her a transmitter and her phone could solve the never-ending bickering between her and Killian about the radio stations. He'd tried. Emma was old-school. She liked her yellow VW bug, and she liked her radio presets—even if it did mean reprogramming them every time Killian was alone in her car long enough to change them.

"I'm ready if you are," Henry said.

"You sure you have everything you need for tonight?" Regina asked. "Your toothbrush? Your suit for the dinner cruise? Clean underwear?"

Henry's face warmed with embarrassment. Why did his parents insist on acting like he was still a kid? "I've got everything, Mom. Geez."

"I'm just checking," she said, leaning in to give him a hug.

He submitted to a kiss on the cheek and then he and Emma headed for the car parked next to the curb.

The sky was just beginning to lighten in the east, and there was a hushed quality in the air as the world hovered between day and night. Henry was almost floating with the possibility of the day ahead.

"Don't even try to pretend you didn't change all the stations," Emma said to Killian when she got in the driver's seat.

"Who, me?" Killian said with a grin.

Henry rolled down the window as Emma started the car. The whole day stretched in front of him. He was going to help Violet get her father's notebook. After that, they would hit as many of the city's cheesy, touristy, romantic landmarks as they could before they were forced to rejoin the rest of Storybrooke High's junior class for more cheesy touristy landmarks. By this time next week, Sir Morgan would be his old self, and Henry and Violet would be closer than ever.

Three

The parking lot was crowded with parents and students when Violet's father pulled into one of the empty spots. A big tour bus stood at the curb and Violet could make out the shadows of the kids who were already moving down the aisle to claim the best seats. The air was filled with the electricity of expectation, a low hum traveling over the blacktop as everyone chatted excitedly about the day ahead.

"Thank you for the ride," Violet said, leaning over to kiss her father on the cheek.

She would have preferred to drive herself, but he wasn't exactly enthusiastic about letting her behind the wheel. She was half surprised he didn't make her ride Nicodemus to get around. She'd been lucky to get a license at all.

"Would you like me to stay until you leave?" he asked.

"It's okay," she said. "I'm going to get on the bus anyway."

He nodded. "Be careful, Violet. And call when you're on your way home."

Her father didn't use a cell phone, but he never failed to pick up the landline when she called.

"I will."

She slipped out of the car and closed the door, then offered him a last wave before turning toward the crowd. Storybrooke High wasn't a very big school, but it was still hard to spot people she knew with everyone all jumbled together. It was a sea of parents and teachers, students and their younger siblings in pajamas who had been roused out of bed for the early morning drop-off.

Her instinct was to look for Henry first, and she scanned the crowd, searching for his brown hair and the corduroy jacket he wore almost everywhere.

There were Mr. Blankenship and Miss Pond, talking to the bus driver near Henry's grandmother, who was looking down at a clipboard. A few feet away, Lizette and Sadie, Violet's best friends and roommates for the overnight trip, were standing by the bus, Lizette on her phone while Sadie sifted through her bag. Violet was starting to wonder if Henry was running late when she spotted him standing between Emma and Killian.

His eyes lit up when he saw her, and she waited as he started across the blacktop. She brushed off the sense of relief that washed over her as he got closer. Most of the kids in Storybrooke had grown up together. It was natural to feel a little out of place, even after a couple of years. There was nothing wrong with relying on Henry.

"Hi," she said when he reached her.

He smiled and bent to kiss her cheek, then glanced around. "Hi."

She laughed. PDA was discouraged at school, but really he was looking for her father. "He already left."

Henry reached out and took her overnight bag, lowering his voice as he leaned toward her. "Is it still there?"

She nodded, knowing he was referring to the notebook. "I checked before I left the house. It's still on the website."

He'd been the one who showed her how to set up alerts with search strings that might indicate her father's notebook for sale. She'd begun to think it was nothing but a fantasy, that the book had been lost or destroyed somewhere in the past hundred and fifty years, when she'd gotten an alert on the listing at Back in the Day. Henry had been the first person she'd told.

"And you're sure we shouldn't call first?" he asked her now. "See how much it is?"

"I'm sure. If it's out of my price range, I won't have any leverage on the phone."

"Yeah, but it's going to be hard to use the family card in person," Henry said. "You look a little young to have a father who was alive in 1887."

"I've already thought about that. I'll say Hank Morgan is an ancestor. I can't prove it, but it will still be easier to convince someone when we're face to face."

Now that she'd said it out loud, she wasn't so sure. Maybe Henry was right. What if they got all the way to the antiques store and she couldn't afford the notebook? The price wasn't listed on the website. If it was more than she'd saved, she would have to resort to convincing the seller she had an attachment to a distant ancestor.

Not exactly common for someone her age.

Plus, antiques dealers were businesspeople. It wasn't as though they would give it to her at a discount simply because they felt sorry for her.

Henry took her hand. "You're probably right. Come on."

Doubt was still echoing in her mind as he led her through the crowd toward Emma and Killian.

"Good morning!" Emma said when she spotted them.

"Good morning," Violet said.

Violet liked both of Henry's moms and made a point to remind him how lucky he was when he got annoyed with them. Her mother had died when Violet was young, and Violet had no memory of her at all. She couldn't imagine what it was like to have not one but two mothers. On the other hand, she had her father, and she wouldn't have traded him for anything in the world, even when he was grumpy or sad.

"Ready to take a bite out of the Big Apple?" Killian asked her with a grin.

Emma rolled her eyes. "I hope you're ready for lots of bad jokes, too."

Violet smiled. "I'm ready for both."

"Good answer," Killian said with a wink.

"Emma!" They turned in unison to see Mary Margaret hurrying toward them. She looked down at the clipboard in her hands and blew her hair out of her eyes. "Someone miscounted. We have eight more kids than we expected."

"Stowaways, eh?" Killian asked.

Mary Margaret didn't look amused. "Can you take two more in your group?"

"No problem," Emma said. "Just tell me who not to lose and we won't lose them."

Violet had to force herself not to cringe. Emma and Killian would be held responsible when she and Henry snuck off to get her father's notebook. It wasn't fair to them, and it wasn't fair to Henry, either. He would get in a lot of trouble. She wondered if he would let her go alone, then quickly discounted the idea. Henry would never agree, and she wasn't entirely sure she could navigate the city without him. It was a once-in-a-lifetime opportunity to get her father's notebook. She would just have to apologize after the fact and hope that Emma, Killian, and Mary Margaret would understand once she explained the reason for their escape.

"Great," Mary Margaret said. She pulled a piece of paper off the clipboard and handed it to Emma. "You have six kids. No food allergies or special needs that we know of."

Emma looked down at the list. "Got it."

Mary Margaret took a deep breath and seemed to see Henry and Violet for the first time.

"Hi, Henry." She touched his head and smiled at Violet. "Hello, Violet. How's your father?"

"He's well, thank you," Violet said. "He said to tell you all hello."

"We should probably get our seat before all the good ones are taken," Henry said, lifting his duffel bag off the pavement near Emma's feet.

"That sounds good," Violet said.

Henry turned to his family. "See you on the bus."

Emma raised her eyebrows. "Blowing us off in record time."

Violet wanted to apologize for Henry but he was already leading her toward the bus.

"Don't you think we should sit with your parents?" she asked as Henry dropped their overnight bags on the pavement with the others that would be stowed under the bus.

"What? No way," Henry said. "They're great and everything, but the whole point of today is to ditch the twenty-four-hour surveillance."

She followed him up the stairs of the bus and down the narrow aisle, watching him consider the open seats. "And that's what we're going to do when we get there," Violet pressed. "We could at least keep them company on the drive."

He chose an empty seat in the middle of the bus and stepped aside so she could have the window. "If it will make you feel better, I'll sit with them for some of the ride."

"I'm sure your mom would appreciate it," Violet said, sliding into the seat.

They got settled and Violet watched through the window as everyone else started moving toward the bus. Now that she'd talked to Emma, Killian, and Mary Margaret, she felt less certain about her plan. What if they weren't able to slip away at all? Emma was bound to stick close to Henry, and Mary Margaret clearly took seriously her job as a fill-in organizer for Mrs. Holt.

She turned to Henry. "What if we can't get away?"

He took her hand and smiled. "Don't worry. We'll do it right after we get off the bus, when the teachers and chaperones are getting organized. That'll be our best chance."

She still wasn't sure, but his confidence was comforting and she smiled as he leaned in to give her a quick kiss. He was probably right. He usually was.

Four

The sun was just beginning to climb into the sky when Violet dozed off with her head against the window. Looking at her, Henry felt like the luckiest guy in the world. Violet was beautiful and smart and kind—everything anybody could ever want in someone—and she was his girlfriend. He didn't know what he'd done to deserve her, but he intended to keep proving he was worthy.

He pulled out his phone as it buzzed in his pocket and smiled at the text from his mom.

I CAN'T TAKE ANY MORE BIG APPLE JOKES. TAKE PITY ON ME?

Emma and Killian adored each other. The gleam in Killian's eyes when he managed to push Emma's buttons was matched only by Emma's when she made fun of Killian's jokes. Their bickering was just part of the routine.

He pulled the cardigan Violet was using as a blanket around her shoulders and eased out of the seat.

Most of the kids were sleeping, listening to music, or watching videos on their phones as he made his way toward the back of the bus, where Emma sat with Killian. He lifted a hand in greeting to his friends Drew Kasinsky and Paul Sabatini, his roommates for the trip, as he passed their seats, trying to remember when he'd last hung out with them. It wasn't as easy as it should have been; he spent most of his time with Violet now.

His mother looked up at him and mouthed the words *Help me* as he approached. He shook his head and tried not to laugh as he balanced on the end of the seat she was sharing with Killian.

"How's the ride so far?" his mom asked.

"It's fine," he said. "Violet's out."

"I'm not surprised. No civilized person should have to get up as early as we did today."

Henry was glad they'd left as early as they had, even though it meant getting up in the dark. It would give him and Violet more time alone together in the city.

"You're not going to get an argument from me," he said.

"We haven't been able to talk much lately," Emma said. "You've been so busy studying for finals."

"One more month until summer," he said.

Just saying it made him happy. Two and a half months to sleep in and stay up late, to get ice cream and swim with Violet.

"Have you thought about next year?" Emma asked. "Maybe we should start planning some college visits or something?"

The uncertainty in her voice made him feel a little better about his own. Regina always had everything figured out. It was nice when you wanted someone to take control, but not so nice when you needed space to figure things out on your own. Emma was never shy about admitting she wasn't a natural at the whole parenting thing. The fact that she was as out of her element thinking about Henry's future as he was made him feel less embarrassed about his indecision.

"I don't know," he said. "I'm not even sure I want to go to college."

"Do you have something else in mind?"

He thought about it. "Not really. It just feels like I've been in school most of my life."

She smiled. "You have."

"Exactly. College just feels like more of the same."

"College isn't high school," she said. "But I know what you mean."

"I don't know," he admitted. "It would be nice to see something different, to do something really different."

"Maybe you could take a gap year. Volunteer overseas or do some traveling."

He tried to picture himself building houses in some

far-flung country or backpacking through Europe. It didn't really feel like him.

"Maybe," he said anyway.

"What are Violet's plans?" she asked.

"She wants to go to college, but she's worried about her dad," Henry said.

She nodded. "That's a tough one, but I'm sure Hank would manage."

"I don't know, he hasn't been doing too well." Henry hesitated, imagining Violet far away at school while he did . . . what exactly?

She looked at him like she knew he'd left something unsaid. "And?"

Sometimes it was annoying that his moms knew him so well.

"What would happen to Violet and me if she went to college and I stayed in Storybrooke or went somewhere else?"

She tipped her head. "I don't know, but I do know you can't make decisions about your future based on

Violet, and she can't make decisions for herself based on what you decide to do. You each have to do what's best for yourselves and trust things will work out the way they're meant to. I know that sounds like a lame grown-up thing to say, but it's true."

"But I love her." The confession made his cheeks burn. He'd never actually said it to anyone but Violet.

His mom put her arm around him. "I hate to be the one to tell you this, kid, but not everything is meant to last forever."

He looked toward the front of the bus. He could just make out Violet's dark hair, her head still propped up by the window. He knew her cheeks would be slightly flushed, her lips parted, chest rising and falling with her breath while she slept.

His mom meant well, but she didn't understand how he and Violet felt about each other. Maybe it was true that not everything was meant to last forever, but he and Violet were.

He just knew it.

Five

Violet could hardly pull her eyes away from the window as they moved through the city. She'd slept for a couple of hours after they'd left Storybrooke, but now her nerves were humming with excitement. She watched with fascination as people rushed to and fro on the sidewalks, walking with purpose toward some unknown destination. Skyscrapers gleamed far above them in the morning sun, and she craned her neck, trying to see to the top through the limited view of the small window.

It was like being in another world, one where everyone was sharply dressed and on their way somewhere important and exciting. The cacophony was muffled through the walls of the bus, but she still felt a thrill hearing the sound of car horns and construction work echo across the pavement.

She wasn't the only one who felt it. The chatter on the bus had grown more and more excited as they approached the city, her classmates jostling for position in front of the windows. Even Lizette seemed enraptured by the scene, her phone nowhere in sight.

"Remember," Henry said next to her, "we have to make a break for it right when we get off the bus. Once we start to board the ferry, it will be too late."

"I remember."

She was still nervous, but now that they were in the city, she was excited, too. The opportunity to be part of the hum and excitement on the other side of the glass was too good to pass up.

The bus made a sharp turn and the water came into view, the Statue of Liberty shining in the sun like a beacon, torch raised proudly skyward.

"Look. . . ."

"There it is!"

"Move so I can take a picture. . . ."

Violet was glad she and Henry were on the right side of the bus to have a view of the water.

"Do you want to sit by the window so you can see it better?" she asked Henry.

He smiled and met her eyes. "No, thanks. I have the best view of all."

Her cheeks grew warm with the compliment, butterflies taking flight in her stomach. They were really going to do it. She and Henry were going to ditch the class and spend the day alone getting her father's notebook. They would miss the wax museum, but they should have the notebook in hand in time to rejoin the group at Chelsea Piers for bowling, followed by a romantic dinner cruise on the Hudson. The next day they would go to the Met with their classmates before heading back to Storybrooke in the afternoon.

Even the prospect of angering Emma and Killian with their escape couldn't dampen her excitement.

Battery Park came into view and their bus pulled behind a row of other buses, all lined up to dispatch their cargo onto the pavement. Beyond the park's sidewalks, boats dotted the water like confetti. Some were ferries making their way toward the Statue of Liberty and Ellis Island, the same itinerary planned for the students of Storybrooke. Others were private vessels heading out onto the vast open water. Those were the seafarers Violet envied most, those unseen people on adventures all their own.

The fierceness of her desire for freedom took her by surprise. She'd gotten so used to being in Storybrooke that it was easy to forget there was more to the world. The realization was both terrifying and thrilling. She was glad when the bus reached the drop-off point and everyone stood to disembark. Some things were too complicated to figure out at ten in the morning.

"Ready?" Henry asked her as he stood to exit the bus.

She took a deep breath. "I think so."

"It'll be okay. Just follow my lead."

She grabbed her bag and followed him down the aisle. Their overnight bags would remain on the bus until they were dropped off at the hotel after the wax museum and bowling at Chelsea Piers. Henry and Violet would be back with the group way before then.

They stepped onto the concrete and moved away from the entrance of the bus as everyone else exited. Mary Margaret was already on the ground, looking at her clipboard and directing students toward their assigned chaperones for the day.

Violet was watching for Sadie and Lizette when she heard a voice carrying over the sidewalk. She turned to see a man in a hat and tweed suit standing with his back to the line of buses as he gestured dramatically toward the water beyond the park.

"You may grow old and trembling in your anatomies, you may lie awake at night listening to the disorder of your veins, you may miss your only love, you may see the world about you devastated by evil lunatics, or know your honor trampled in the sewers of baser minds. There is only one thing for it then—to learn."

She was entranced by his voice, loud and commanding as he seemed to perform for the Statue of Liberty in the distance. She watched with fascination as he turned to face them, his hat pulled down too far over his face for her to get a good look at his features. He continued speaking, the sun glinting off his shoes.

"Learn why the world wags and what wags it. That is the only thing which the mind can never exhaust, never alienate, never be tortured by, never fear or distrust, and never dream of regretting," he recited. "Learning is the only thing for you. Look what a lot of things there are to learn."

"People here are crazy, am I right?"

Lizette's voice pulled Violet's attention away from the man's performance.

"I don't know," Violet said. "Maybe he's an actor rehearsing his lines or something."

"Or a spy sending a secret message to someone in code," Sadie suggested in a dramatic voice.

Lizette rolled her eyes. "Let's be honest; crazy is the most likely scenario."

"What's crazy is this view," Sadie said, her eyes pulled to the water. She was small and blond, her hair shaped into a pixie cut that made her look like a fairy princess.

"It's amazing," Violet said.

"I hope I don't get seasick," Lizette said.

Sadie pulled a small tube from her bag. "I have Dramamine if you need it."

"I'll pass," Lizette said, pulling her brown hair into a messy bun. "My mom gave it to me when we went on that class trip to Boston. I was a zombie the whole day. I don't even remember most of it."

Sadie dropped the tube in her bag. "Never mind."

Everyone laughed.

"I think we're with Mr. Dalton," Lizette said. "I guess you're with Henry and his mom?"

"That's right," Violet said.

Lizette pouted. "Too bad. We never see you anymore."

Lizette and Sadie had been Violet's first friends in Storybrooke after Henry. It had been a revelation: the sleepovers at Lizette's when they would stay up late talking about boys; the Saturday afternoons they spent giggling in the dark at the Storybrooke Movie Theater;

all the hours they spent shopping, Lizette and Sadie encouraging Violet to try on an assortment of clothing that made her head spin.

Lizette was right. It had been a long time.

"We'll plan something when we get home," Violet promised. "And at least we have tonight at the hotel. It'll be just like old times."

"Minus my mom's cooking," Lizette said.

"Thank god." Sadie laughed.

Lizette's mom loved watching cooking shows and using the girls to experiment. Unfortunately, her enthusiasm usually didn't translate into actual skill, and Sadie and Violet had gotten good at smuggling in snacks to gorge on after Lizette's parents went to bed.

"Lizette, Sadie!" Mary Margaret called to them from behind her clipboard.

"That's us," Lizette said. "See you on the boat."

Violet watched them make their way to Mary Margaret, wondering why she felt a sinking feeling in the pit of her stomach. Then Henry took her hand, and she remembered she had the whole day with him to look forward to. She missed Lizette and Sadie, but they were still friends. Their night at the hotel would be a good way to begin rebuilding their old closeness.

She was pulled from her thoughts by the arrival of Emma and Killian, the last ones off the bus.

"Come on," Emma said. "Let's go pick up the rest of our crew."

They threaded their way through the crowd toward Mary Margaret. She was calling out names, assigning kids to their chaperones, the students listening carefully in spite of the chaos. Violet couldn't help admiring Mary Margaret's authority. She was always in the thick of things, taking control and making decisions. Violet hoped someday she would be able to command such respect.

"Emma and Killian?" Mary Margaret said.

"Right here," Emma said.

Mary Margaret used the pen in her hand to touch names on her list. "Ruth Beaumont, Jackson Keen, Matthew Derry, and Melody Summerfield, you're with Emma and Killian. Plus Henry and Violet, of course."

Unlike their roommates at the hotel, whom they'd

been able to choose, group assignments for sightseeing had been randomly selected. Violet thought it had something to do with forcing them to expand their horizons.

She didn't mind. It was a good group. Jack and Matthew were in her precalculus class, and she'd gotten to know Ruth the year before in gym. Melody was new to the school, but Violet always saw her reading in the halls and at lunch. She had a feeling they could be friends. They were all going to have a great day together and she felt a twinge of regret when she remembered that she and Henry wouldn't be part of most of it.

"Hi," Ruth said, coming over to stand near Violet.

Violet smiled at her. "Hi."

"I'm so excited," Ruth said, tucking a piece of curly blond hair behind one ear. "I've never even seen the Statue of Liberty or Ellis Island up close."

"Me neither," Violet said. "And it's such a nice day to be on the water."

"It really is," Ruth said, looking up at the sky with a smile.

Doubt once again seeped in around Violet's excitement. She hoped the rest of the group wouldn't suffer when Emma and Killian realized she and Henry were gone. Would the students in their group be reassigned to other chaperones? She hoped they wouldn't miss any of the sights because of her and Henry.

She was starting to think this was a bad idea. Maybe there was a better way to get her father's notebook.

She looked at Henry, trying to find a way to signal her doubt.

"Okay, everyone, let's move toward the ferry terminal," Mary Margaret called out. "Stay in your groups, please."

It was too late. They were moving toward the hulking steel-and-glass terminal on the water. She was carried along by the crowd, pressed too closely together to say anything without everyone around them hearing it.

Ready or not, their plan was already in action. There was no going back now.

Six

Henry looked over the crowd as they headed toward the ferry terminal. He hadn't expected to be quite so close to everyone else. They were taking Mary Margaret's instructions seriously, staying together in their groups with their chaperones. He hoped they would spread out a little once they got inside the terminal, otherwise it was going to be pretty hard to sneak away without alerting everyone around them—including his mom and Killian.

Violet was quiet as everyone else talked excitedly. He reached over and took her hand, hoping to reassure her. She looked up at him with a nervous smile and his feelings for her spread like sunshine through his chest. They were a long way from their quiet days at school and around the small town they called home. It was up to him to make sure she felt safe and confident in the eventual success of their mission.

"You ever been here before?" Jack asked, next to him.

Henry had known Jack since third grade. They'd never been close friends, but Henry liked him well enough.

"Sure," Henry said. "How about you?"

"Once," Jack said, readjusting the backpack on his lanky frame. "But it was a long time ago."

"I'm sure you'll have a great time," Henry said.

"And you won't?" Jack said.

Henry hadn't been paying close attention. He had the feeling he'd missed something important. "What do you mean?"

Jack laughed and shook his head. "You said I'd have a great time. It almost sounds like you don't plan to have fun, too."

"Right!" Henry wondered if he sounded as nervous as he felt. "I definitely plan on having a good time."

They stepped into the shadow of the ferry terminal and the temperature dropped a few degrees. Henry took a last look at the street beyond the park, wanting to have a plan when he and Violet emerged. He should have checked for the nearest subway station before they'd gotten to the city. They would have to move quickly, disappear into the crowd, and get underground before they were spotted by anyone from Storybrooke.

"Okay, everyone, line up to get on the ferry," Mary Margaret called out.

Their group followed her instructions, taking their places at the back of a line next to the water. There was naked desperation in Violet's eyes as they got into line behind Jack and in front of Killian. He was glad his mom was heading up the front of the line. It would be harder to slip away from her than from Killian, who was prone to distraction.

Henry smiled to ease Violet's worry as he tried to

cover his own panic. He hadn't expected everything to move so fast. They'd been off the bus less than ten minutes and they were already in line for the ferry. There had been no fumbling by the teachers or chaperones, no rogue groups of students wandering off that might have offered a distraction.

In other words, everything had gone according to plan—just not *their* plan.

"What do we do?" Violet said under her breath.

"I don't know," Henry said. "We'll think of something."

But he wasn't so sure. Water lapped against the terminal to their right, and the line stretched both in front of them and behind them.

He eyed the wide expanse of concrete to their left. Tourists milled back and forth, but not enough to offer any real cover. They would have to bolt from the line and across the concrete, and he wasn't at all sure Emma and Killian wouldn't catch them, even if they were willing to make a scene with their escape.

"Henry, look!" Violet said softly.

He followed the direction of her gaze toward the

front of the line and a wall rising up on the left. Once they hit it, there would be no going back. They would be fed into a narrow channel with the water on one side and the wall on the other, then into the lines formed by metal barricades that would force them onto the boat waiting next to the dock.

And once they were on the boat, their plans would be blown to bits.

He looked frantically for a way out.

Killian turned around in line, his eyes directed at the itinerary in his hands. "Looks like a cruise around Lady Liberty, then a quick tour of Ellis," he said, looking up at the group. "I have to admit I'm glad I arrived here the way I did. I don't fancy a trip through immigration."

Violet smiled, but Henry could see the worry in her eyes as the line inched forward.

Killian was still facing them as he studied the second page of the itinerary.

Turn around, Henry thought. *Look the other way just for a minute.*

A moment later, he knew it was pointless as his mom

left her place in line to count the six people in their group. By the time she returned to the front of the group, the wall was upon them. A moment later, they stepped into its shadow, the metal barricades ahead.

"Henry . . ."

He looked down at Violet. "I know. Don't worry. We'll figure something out."

The line moved faster, everyone picking up the pace as more people boarded the ferry up ahead. Melody held a book in front of her, reading even when the line came to a brief stop, while Jake and Noah scrolled on their phones. Ruth gazed out over the water and Violet clutched Henry's hand as they moved with the crowd.

For a moment, Henry thought they might get a reprieve. The boat looked crowded, the passengers on the lower deck one big shadow, more passengers quickly filling the upper deck. Maybe they wouldn't make it onto this boat and they'd have to wait for another one. There would still be the concrete wall to deal with, but at least they wouldn't be out on the water, heading farther away from the city by the minute.

Then he saw Miss Pond leading the way up the ramp to the ferry and he knew they were doomed. There was no way the Storybrooke group would be separated. If one of them was on this ferry, the rest of them would be, too.

Defeat sat like a boulder on his chest as they made their way through the metal barricades toward the boat, his day alone with Violet receding like an impossible dream.

"I'm sorry," he said as they stepped onto the ramp.

She sighed. "It's okay. It's early. We'll figure something out."

They boarded behind the rest of the crowd, Emma and Killian herding them together up a set of stairs to the bridge of the boat. Then they were high above the water, the Statue of Liberty beckoning in the distance— and the city they were supposed to be moving through as far away as ever.

Seven

Violet was filled with despair as the boat chugged out to sea. Less than an hour before, she'd envied those who were on the water. Now all she could think about was her father's sad eyes. His notebook was as close as it would ever be and yet so out of reach it might as well have been on the moon.

She held on to the railing to keep her balance as she followed Henry to the back of the boat. They leaned against the metal railing, watching the city get smaller behind them.

"Well, that didn't go as planned," Violet said.

"I think that was the problem," Henry said. "We didn't really have a plan. I'm sorry."

She put her hand over his on the railing. "This is my idea, and it's my father's notebook we're after. I should have come up with a plan."

She knew it was true as soon as she said it. Why did she always assume everything would work out even when she didn't do anything to make sure it did? Even in Camelot, nothing fell magically into place. Of course, she'd thought everything had at the time, but that's because she'd been a child.

She had no such excuse now. She wasn't a child anymore. She knew that when things went right it was because someone made sure they went right, yet she still too often waited for someone else to ensure that they did.

Henry turned toward her and looked around for the chaperones before leaning down to kiss her quickly on the lips. "It might have been your plan, but it's our mission. I could have come up with something, too."

"Do you think it's too late?" she asked.

"I don't know." His gaze drifted across the water to the city, its noise lost to the rush of wind and the sound of the boat slicing through the waves. "We're not stopping at Liberty Island. The itinerary says we'll ride past it, then on to Ellis. We're supposed to be at Chelsea Piers by four p.m., which means we'll have to leave Ellis by twelve-thirty if we want to make it back in time for bowling."

She and Henry had agreed when making their plans that while they might be able to get away with missing the wax museum after the ferry tour, they would be pushing their luck if they weren't back in time for bowling at Chelsea Piers.

She tried to see the movements of their group in her mind—getting on and off the ferry, moving through the ferry terminal to reboard the bus, exiting in another part of the city.

"Maybe when we get back on the bus to go to the wax museum?" Violet suggested. "Or maybe once we get into the museum everyone will spread out and the chaperones will give us more space?"

It would mean cutting short their time alone, but they might still have time to get the notebook.

"Maybe," Henry said. "We'll have to play it by ear, wait for the right moment. Where did you say the antiques shop is again?"

Violet pulled out her phone. "Two sixty-one West Fourth Street."

Henry seemed to think about it. "As long as we get there by two p.m. or so, we should still have time to get the notebook and meet up with the group for bowling before the dinner cruise."

"That gives us a little under three hours to find a way to escape," Violet said.

Henry nodded. "We'll make it work."

The boat's intercom crackled to life, the voice of the announcer distorted as she pointed out the Statue of Liberty on their right. Violet glanced over and nearly lost her breath; as impressive as Lady Liberty was from land, it didn't compare to her majesty up close.

She rose from the water like a peaceful warrior, the

sun shining on her crown, her torch held high for all to see. Violet thought about everything she'd learned in U.S. History at school, seeing in her mind's eye all the people who must have been greeted by the statue when they arrived in America. She was surprised to feel her throat choke with emotion. She'd been so caught up worrying about the notebook that she'd forgotten to appreciate what was right in front of her.

The boat's passengers had grown quiet, as if everyone was equally moved by the sight. For a moment there was nothing but the sound of the wind, the water under the boat, and the quiet clicking of cameras as everyone took pictures.

Violet looked up at Henry. He smiled and reached over for her hand, the moment settling between them. She suddenly wasn't quite as sorry they'd been unable to sneak away at the ferry terminal. Whatever happened with her father's notebook, she was glad she'd been part of the magic on the boat when hundreds of people had been rendered silent by history brought to life.

Henry's gaze was pulled from hers as the boat cleared the statue. She followed his eyes to the next island looming in front of them.

"That's Ellis," he said.

She shrugged, her earlier worry about sneaking away eased by the moment they'd shared. "Unless you have an idea that doesn't involve swimming back to shore, we might as well enjoy it."

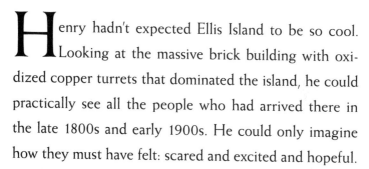

Eight

Henry hadn't expected Ellis Island to be so cool. Looking at the massive brick building with oxidized copper turrets that dominated the island, he could practically see all the people who had arrived there in the late 1800s and early 1900s. He could only imagine how they must have felt: scared and excited and hopeful.

He was still mad at himself for not having a plan to get away from the group, but the moment he'd shared with Violet as they'd cruised past the Statue of Liberty had made it worth it. They would figure something out. In the meantime, they would make the best of it by enjoying the time they had to explore.

The boat slowed as it approached the dock on the island. Emma waved him over, and he and Violet threaded their way through the crowd already making its way toward the stairs.

Emma's eyes were sparkling, a smile lighting up her face. "How awesome was that?"

Henry didn't even have to humor her when it came to the Statue of Liberty. "It was pretty awesome."

"It was beautiful," Violet said. "I didn't expect it to be so big up close."

"Well, get ready to have your mind blown again," Emma said. "Ellis is just as amazing."

Henry spotted the back of Killian's head as they joined the crowd trying to get down the stairs. Matthew's backpack bobbed next to him, Melody's ponytail swishing against her jacket.

For a few minutes, there was nothing but the press of bodies and the slow shuffle of their feet as they inched down the narrow staircase and onto the first level of the boat. Then they were stepping out into the sunshine amid the cry of seagulls circling overhead.

They made their way through the throng toward his grandma, her clipboard in hand as she did a head count. The chaperones stood with their groups as Mary Margaret ticked names off the field trip manifest.

"This place is huge!" Killian looked at the map that had been given to all the chaperones. "We only have two hours here. We need a plan."

Emma moved closer to him, leaning over to look at the map. "Let's start on the first floor and make our way around and up to the second. We'll let the kids decide how long to spend on each exhibit. We can catch one of the documentary showings along the way."

Killian put his arm around Emma and winked. "As long as I get to hold your hand in the dark."

She laughed and shook her head.

Henry smiled and tried to imagine him and Violet in twenty years. Would they be silly and playful like his mom and Killian? Or would they be serious but sweet? He didn't know, but he liked thinking about it, him and Violet still together.

"Emma?" Mary Margaret called out.

"Over here."

"Are all six of your kids accounted for?" Mary Margaret asked, pen poised over her clipboard.

Emma did a quick scan of their group. "I've got them."

Henry's cheek's heated when he imagined his mom realizing he and Violet were gone. Even if they'd managed to get away in the ferry terminal, she would have realized they were missing before they got on the boat. There would have been a frantic search and Emma and Killian would have had to stay behind to look for them.

He was glad they were there for the count now, but there was no denying it: if he and Violet managed to get away at some point, his mom was going to look around and realize they were gone. He didn't like the thought of her worrying or having to answer for the fact that he and Violet had gone missing. He would text her at the first opportunity and explain.

"That's everyone," Mary Margaret said, glancing at Mr. Blankenship.

"We have two hours until our ferry leaves," Mr.

Blankenship called out. "Stay with your group during that time and meet back here to board the boat. And of course, we expect all of you to be respectful as you represent Storybrooke High."

His mom turned to the group. "What do you say? You guys ready to explore this place?"

"Ready," Matthew said.

They stepped under a long canopy leading to the main building and followed the crowd through the big glass doors. The central hall was long and wide, with a massive tiled ceiling that curved like a barrel looming two stories over their heads. Henry recognized some of his classmates already making their way around the second floor walkway above them.

"Um, is there any way I can go to the bathroom before we get started?" Melody asked Emma.

"Of course." Emma turned to Killian. "Do you have the map?"

Killian handed it to her and she studied it for a few seconds before giving it back.

"Over by the café," she said. "This way."

Henry glanced at the exhibits as they made their way through the big hall. Ellis Island looked every bit as cool as the Statue of Liberty. He was glad he'd get to explore it with Violet in spite of the fact that their plans to get the notebook had been delayed.

They entered a wide hall crowded with people. His stomach growled as the scent of cooking meat and hot oil reached his nose. It felt like ages since he and Violet had been on the bus, sharing the snacks Regina prepared for them.

"Let's meet back here in five minutes," Emma said, heading into the bathroom with Ruth and Melody.

"Take advantage of it while you can, boys," Killian said.

Jack and Matthew followed him into the men's room, leaving Henry and Violet standing in the hall.

"Want to take a look?" Violet asked, her eyes on the glass doors at the end of the hall.

Henry followed her gaze. Beyond the doors, a

concrete terrace stretched toward the lawn, and beyond it, the water.

"Sure!" Henry looked at his phone to mark the time as they headed for the door.

They stepped out into sunshine amid the chatter of other tourists who gathered by the railing overlooking the water. Light glinted off the ocean, two ferries passing in the distance as they made the eternal loop to and from the terminal to Liberty and Ellis islands. The salty scent of the sea was thick in the air and Violet inhaled deeply, a smile spreading across her face.

"Isn't it lovely?" she asked, closing her eyes.

He watched as she smiled into the sun, her long hair blowing back in the wind. "It is," he said. "And so are you."

She opened her eyes and looked up at him with a smile. "You're a sweet-talker, Henry Mills."

"I mean every word." He crossed his heart with his index finger.

Movement behind her caught his eye and he leaned back to get a better view. She followed his gaze to a ferry at the dock. He didn't know if it was the same one they'd taken to Ellis—they all looked the same to him—but it was taking on passengers for the trip back to the city. He'd known multiple ferries made the trip back and forth to Liberty and Ellis islands, but it had never occurred to him that the schedule allowed for another way to escape the group.

"Are you thinking what I'm thinking?" Violet asked, still looking at the boat.

"Yep," Henry said.

It seemed worse somehow, skipping out on his mom and the rest of the group when they were on the island, like they would be taking advantage of its distance from the city. He wondered if it would make his mom worry even more.

"Hey! What are you guys doing out here?"

Henry turned to see Lizette and Sadie hurrying toward them.

"Um . . . just waiting for the rest of the group," Violet said. "They're in the bathroom."

"You have to stay with your group?" Lizette asked, positioning herself in front of the railing and holding out her phone to take a picture of herself in front of the water.

"That's the plan," Henry said, his eyes shifting to the ferry, its top level slowly filling with people.

"Mr. and Mrs. Rutherford told us we could do our own thing," Lizette said, head bowed to her phone as she added a filter to the photograph.

"Sounds great," Henry said.

He shifted his gaze to the ferry. The boat was still at the dock, the line empty. It was early. Most tourists were just starting their sightseeing for the day, not heading back to the city.

Violet met his eyes and a moment of understanding seemed to pass between them. He reached for her hand and looked at Lizette and Sadie.

"Hey, Sadie, can you do me a favor?" Henry asked.

"Um, sure?" she said.

He started edging away from them toward a small

concrete staircase that led to the lawn. "Can you tell my mom not to worry? That we have something to do but will catch up later?"

"Wait, what do you mean?" Lizette asked. "Where are you going?"

"We just have something we have to do," Henry said. "Can you tell her?"

"I mean, yeah, I'll tell her," Sadie said. "But don't you think she's going to be mad?"

Henry nodded. "Probably. Just promise you'll tell her. She'll be out of the bathroom by the café in just a minute."

"I promise," Sadie said.

"Thanks."

He guided Violet down the staircase, his heart hammering wildly in his chest.

"Tell her we're sorry," Violet called over her shoulder. "Tell her we'll be okay."

Henry pulled her across the lawn, half expecting to hear his mom shouting his name as they got closer to the boat. Time seemed to slow down, and they stepped onto the boat and hurried to the back of the first level. They would be too visible on the top deck if his mom got the message before they pulled away from the dock. In the meantime, it was possible she would think Sadie's message meant he and Violet were still somewhere on Ellis Island, exploring on their own.

"Are you sure you want to do this?" Violet asked.

Henry looked at her as the engines roared to life under the boat. "I'm sure—and it's too late now anyway."

The boat shifted under their feet as it pulled away from the dock.

"Come on," he said. "Let's go upstairs."

He tried to sound lighthearted about what they were doing, but inside all he could see was his mom's face when Sadie told her they were gone.

Nine

Violet forced herself not to look back as the ferry headed for the mainland. Escaping the group had seemed less extreme when she'd thought about slipping away at the ferry terminal. It seemed worse somehow to leave the island. Despite the message they'd given Sadie, Emma would worry. She'd be trapped on the island until the next boat left, and even then, she'd have no idea where to find them. Violet wondered how long it would take for Henry's phone to start ringing.

She looked up at Henry as they approached the dock at the ferry terminal and was surprised to find him smiling.

"Do you know something I don't?" she asked. "Because I'm pretty nervous right now."

He took her face in his hands and kissed her. "Just that we're alone in New York City. Finally."

She didn't want to ruin his fun, but it was hard not to think about Emma and Killian and the others. "I wish I could be as excited."

"Listen," he said, still holding her face as he looked into her eyes, "it's done. We can't change it now. Sadie will tell them we're okay and I'll text my mom soon to check in. We're both going to be grounded for life, so we might as well enjoy our freedom while we can."

She took a deep breath. "You have a point."

"Besides, we're finally going to get your father's notebook," he said.

The boat pulled up next to the dock and everyone started moving for the exit.

"You're right." She smiled. "Let the adventure begin."

He bowed at the waist then extended his arm. "My lady."

She laughed and took his hand. Adrenaline pumped through her body as they hurried down the ramp. Violet shouted apologies behind her as they weaved through the crowd. They hit the ground running and continued through the terminal, passing tourists in line for the next ferry trip.

She was gasping for breath when they exited into the park. She pulled Henry to a stop.

"You didn't say anything about a race," she said. "I don't think I can keep up this pace all day."

"Sorry." He looked around. "I'm just trying to get away from the park."

"You think they'll call the terminal and have some-one stop us?" Violet asked. The thought hadn't occurred to her before now.

"I hope the message from Sadie will keep my mom from totally freaking out, but we shouldn't count on it. Come on."

They made their way quickly through the park, past lush gardens strewn with a rainbow of flowers, a bubbling fountain, and a sculpture that looked like a giant golden globe atop a flying person's back. The noise of the city got louder as they approached the street, the honking of cars echoing off the concrete. Skyscrapers rose into the sky, glinting in the sun like towers of mirrors, each reflecting off the other.

They crossed the street and Henry started walking faster.

"There," he said.

She followed his gaze to a staircase that led underground. A sign advertised it as the Bowling Green station.

They headed that direction, walking over large letters drawn in yellow sidewalk chalk on the pavement. She read the message as they passed over it.

THIS WAY.

They hurried down the station stairs, keeping to one side to avoid the people coming up. The smell of hot metal and damp, dirty pavement assaulted her nose as they made their way underground. Screeching sounded somewhere under the street, and a warm wind lifted her hair when they reached the ground.

The subway station was a concrete rectangle filled with people hurrying back and forth from the stairs. Beyond the turnstiles, she could make out the platform. The track in front of it was empty.

Henry looked around, his gaze settling on what looked like a service desk inside a smudged glass cube.

"Let's see if someone in there can help us," he said, leading her toward the booth.

Violet marveled at the ease with which the city crowd ducked and dodged them as they made their way to the booth. They were like modern dancers engaging in an elaborate and perfectly timed routine to get to the turnstiles that led to the trains. They were so vibrant, so alive, so purposeful in their movements. Violet could hardly take her eyes off them. She wanted to know everything. Who were they? Where did they live? Where were they going?

They stepped up to the glass cube and Violet was surprised to see that there was no one in the chair facing the glass. Henry craned his neck, peering into the shadows at the back of the booth as Violet walked around to the side, wondering if there was another room they couldn't see from the front.

There wasn't. It was empty.

"Figures," Henry muttered.

Violet looked around, hoping to spot someone in a uniform. There was no one but the people rushing through the turnstiles. Stopping them for directions seemed about as wise as stepping in front of a charging stallion.

She was about to give up when she spotted something on the far wall of the station.

"Wait!" she said. "What's that?"

Henry followed her eyes toward a wall map lined with grids and colored lines. Graffiti rimmed the edges of the plexiglass that protected it, but it was still obviously a map of the city.

"Nice!" Henry said. "I think that's a subway map. I was about to try my phone, but I have a feeling we're not going to get reception down here."

They stepped back into the crowd to make their way

to the map. She stared at the intersecting lines, some of them thick and some of them thin. It was like no map she had ever seen. Panic clawed its way up her throat. She'd been a fool to think she could do this.

New York City was no Storybrooke.

"We're here," Henry said, pointing to a spot at the end of the island. "What's the address of the antiques shop?"

Violet pulled out her phone and opened her photographs, glad she'd taken a screenshot of the store's address.

"Two sixty-one West Fourth Street," she said.

"Fourth Street . . ." Henry murmured, his eyes scanning the map. "There!"

He pointed to a spot on the map that looked frighteningly far from where they were at the end of the island.

"That far?" Violet asked. "Are you sure?"

"I'm sure," he said. "And it doesn't matter how far it is with the subway. We just have to figure out which one will get us there."

"Those are the colored lines, right?" Violet asked. The longer she stared at the map, the less overwhelming it became.

"Right. So, let's see. . . ."

Violet followed some of the colored lines from where they were at the Bowling Green station, abandoning them when they veered off course from the antiques store. There were so many streets they all started to sound the same after a while.

"This is the one," Henry said, tapping a green line marked with a bold green number four.

Violet stared at the number and the surrounding area. She couldn't put her finger on it, but she had a nagging feeling they were missing something.

"Where is the antiques shop again?" she asked.

Henry pointed to the right of a green square that was labeled as Washington Square Park. "Here."

The bright green line marked with the number four ran right to the area around Henry's finger. A bundle of nerves was still knotted in her stomach, but figuring out why would mean studying the map more carefully when the clock was already ticking on the time they'd been away from the group. Henry knew what he was doing. Henry always knew what he was doing.

"Okay," she said. "The four train it is."

Henry grinned. "Let's go."

They stepped up to the terminal offering Metro-Cards for the subway. Henry loaded one with twenty dollars then handed it to her when they got to the turnstiles.

"You go first and hand it back to me," he said.

She hesitated, hovering over the card reader.

He reached over and adjusted her hand so the magnetic strip was facing the right direction. "Just slide it through."

She followed his instructions and heard a click from inside the turnstile just before she pushed against the metal bar. It gave way and she found herself standing on the other side of it. It was a kind of magic.

Henry reached over the turnstile and she handed

him the card. He followed her through and they stood for a moment, looking at the signs for the trains on both sides of the track. Violet stumbled as someone bumped into her and turned in time to see a slender man in a blue blazer heading for the train idling on one side of the track. She wondered if he'd even seen her. She almost felt invisible, and she was surprised to find it wasn't an entirely unpleasant sensation.

"That's the one," Henry said. "Let's catch it before it leaves."

She looked at the sign for the one on the other side of the track. A crowd was building there but the track was empty. She hesitated, fighting the sudden impulse to go back to the map and double-check their strategy for getting to the antiques store. It would mean crossing back through the exit turnstiles and paying again, but it might be worth it. Once they were on the train, changing direction would be a lot harder.

"What's wrong?" Henry asked.

He was standing a few feet from the open train door.

She glanced back at the other platform, then hurried toward him.

"Nothing," she said. She followed him through the open doors of the train, trying to ignore the feeling that they'd just made a mistake.

Ten

Henry stood next to Violet as the train acceler-
ated out of the station. It was crowded, bodies
packed together inside the train car like sardines in a tin.
He was glad there had been an open seat for Violet. She
had seemed a little overwhelmed by the map. The city
was probably a lot for her to take in after the quiet of
Storybrooke. At least she wouldn't have to endure the
jolts and jerks of the subway standing up.

He scanned the crowd with interest. He'd always figured Storybrooke was exotic, what with all the people
there from other realms, but every time he came to the
city he was reminded all over again that, in a lot of ways,

Storybrooke was like any small town. Everyone knew everyone else—and everyone else's business, too.

There was something appealing about the anonymity of a city. You could be anyone you wanted or no one at all. You didn't have to smile pleasantly and wish everyone good morning for fear of seeming rude. You didn't have to attend every birthday party and anniversary celebration within a five-mile radius. And you definitely didn't have to worry about someone reporting back to your parents if they saw you kiss your girlfriend in public.

He looked down at Violet, wondering why she was so quiet.

He leaned down. "Are you okay?"

"I'm fine." Her voice was short and flat, almost like she was mad at him.

"Are you sure?" he asked.

She smiled up at him but there was something reserved about it. "I'm sure."

He wasn't convinced. Then again, who could blame her for being nervous? Up until now they'd been on the move. There hadn't been time to think too hard about the fact that they'd already been separated from the group for nearly an hour, and were getting farther away from them by the minute.

He pulled his phone out of his pocket. He had to give his mom credit. There were only two texts from her so far.

ARE YOU SERIOUS, KID? WHERE ARE YOU?

THIS ISN'T FUNNY, HENRY. TEXT ME BACK.

He moved to text her back, then realized he didn't have a signal. It was no wonder; they were surrounded by blackness on all sides, the train rocking back and forth on the tracks as they wound their way under the city.

He slipped the phone back in his pocket. At least his mom sounded calm. He would text her back when they were aboveground again.

The train slowed, lights flickering by outside the window as they approached a train platform.

A garbled voice crackled over the loudspeaker. *"Next stop, Wall Street. Wall Street is the next stop."*

He looked down at Violet. "This isn't us."

"I know," she said.

He moved over as some of the passengers shoved past to exit. They were quickly replaced by others getting on at Wall Street. Henry tried to make room.

A moment later, the train started moving again. Henry looked up at the digital readout on the side of the train car. It wasn't a map exactly. More like a timeline of upcoming stops. He tried to visualize the map they'd read on the wall at the Bowling Green station and the name of their stop. He should have taken a picture with his phone. Without a signal there was no way to double-check, and none of the street names on the digital timeline sounded familiar.

He glanced at Violet and decided against asking her if she remembered. There was no point in worrying her by seeming like he didn't know what he was doing. Anyway, the address for the antiques shop had looked a long way from where they had started. They couldn't be close yet, and he was sure he would recognize the name of their stop when he heard it.

"Fulton is the next stop. Next stop, Fulton Street."

The wheels on the train screeched as it came to a stop at the platform. Henry took his phone out of his pocket again, hoping for a signal.

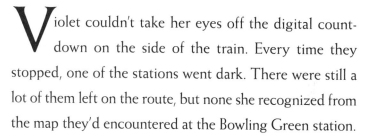

Eleven

Violet couldn't take her eyes off the digital countdown on the side of the train. Every time they stopped, one of the stations went dark. There were still a lot of them left on the route, but none she recognized from the map they'd encountered at the Bowling Green station.

She looked up at Henry, who was studying his phone as they pulled out of the Fulton Street station. She felt bad about snapping at him. He hadn't said a word since their brief conversation when they got on the train and she knew he hadn't totally bought her insistence that she wasn't angry.

And she was angry. She just couldn't figure out why.

It wasn't his fault she'd let him make the decision or that she didn't know which stop was theirs. He hadn't forced her onto the train. If she'd really wanted to take another train or take more time with the map, she should have said something.

She looked out the tinted windows, the underground walls passing by in a darkened blur on the other side, illuminated only occasionally by dim yellow lights when they made a turn. She'd given herself over to disorientation, resigned to the fact that it was impossible to have any sense of time or direction while they hurtled through the tunnels under the city.

It was easy to settle into the rocking of the car, the feeling that they were heading into the unknown at the hands of an unseen driver at the front of the train. It was like traveling at night through the primordial wood in Camelot; there was only the path in front of you and darkness on all sides, except here there were no hooting owls or scurrying small animals. Here there were only the strange unnatural smells, the clang of metal, and the press of bodies all around.

She lost track of the stops for a while and let her mind wander. Each time the train screeched to a halt, the crowd thinned for a few moments, only to be replaced by another as more people boarded. She had no idea how much time had passed when she heard the conductor speak again through the loudspeaker.

"Union Square. Next stop is Union Square."

"This is us," Henry said.

"Are you sure?" she asked.

"I'm sure." The train started to slow. "Come on."

He stepped back to let her in front of him, and she followed the other passengers heading for the doors. The screeching of brakes filled the air as the train came to a stop at a platform just like all the other ones they'd passed since they left the Bowling Green station.

They stepped off the train and Violet followed Henry through the crowd toward a sign marked EXIT.

They ascended a wide concrete staircase amid the increasingly familiar scents of melted rubber, dirty concrete, and hot metal and emerged through a glass shelter onto a busy street.

"Let's see which way we're supposed to go," Henry said, moving back against the shelter to get out of the line of pedestrians while he looked at his phone.

They were on a concrete island between two streets. The sounds of the city were like a song she hadn't realized she'd been missing when they were underground, and she couldn't help smiling as the sound of traffic echoed through the streets. Cars whooshed past, every bit as intent on their destinations as the pedestrians hurrying in every direction, and the smell of cooking peppers from a truck parked near the curb made her mouth water. It was like stepping inside the pages of a magazine or into a fast-paced movie.

Noisy. Overwhelming. Confusing.

But more than anything—exciting.

Storybrooke seemed far away.

Henry looked up from his phone, his gaze on a nearby intersection. "That way."

Violet smiled and gave him a curtsy, suddenly eager to revive the fun in their mission. "After you, my lord."

He laughed and took her hand and they rushed for

the intersection, stepping into the street as a digital clock counted down the seconds until it would again be filled with cars.

Now that they were aboveground and moving, her excitement was back in force. They were in New York City with the whole day and night ahead of them. There would be a price to pay for their abandonment of the group, but Henry was right; they might as well enjoy their freedom while they had it.

Plus, her father's notebook was closer than ever. He was going to be over the moon to have it back. Violet could almost see the happiness that would light his eyes when she gave it to him. She couldn't wait.

They stepped onto the sidewalk and started walking. Life was in full bloom everywhere she looked. They passed little markets and boutiques, bistros and coffee shops. Across the street, a giant metal cube stood on its end like a balancing top, people hurrying past it like it was the most natural thing in the world. Couples held hands and kissed on the sidewalk, and a dapper gentleman walked five tiny dogs. They passed a chicly dressed couple speaking French and a family of tourists taking photographs. Violet watched as a group of students with backpacks walked with their heads down, intent on their conversation.

What would it be like to go to college there? To go to college in any city?

She imagined herself traversing the subways easily and without confusion. She would wear different clothes without anyone asking her about it. She would cut her long hair and no one would care. She would meet people from all over the world and pretend like it was no big deal, like she'd always been worldly and sophisticated instead of small and scared.

She'd played out the whole scenario in her mind before she realized she'd forgotten about Henry. What would happen to them if she went away to college? They hadn't talked specifically about their future, but it seemed to be assumed—by Henry and everyone else in Storybrooke—that they would somehow always be together.

And wasn't that what she wanted? To be with Henry?

She was pulled from her thoughts when Henry came to a stop at the outskirts of a crowd gathered in the middle of a concrete square. A couple was dancing to Tchaikovsky's *Swan Lake*, which drifted through the air from a phone hooked up to a speaker. They were in full costume, the woman in a white leotard and silver tutu, her delicate feet pointed as she pirouetted across the pavement as if it were a grand stage. The young man looked at her with longing, his legs lean and muscular in tights as he lifted her into the air.

Violet looked at Henry and grinned before returning her attention to the magic unfolding in front of her. She could almost see the collective joy of the crowd rising into the air as the music reached a crescendo, the female dancer bending backward as the man held her gracefully in his arms.

"We should go," Henry said.

She nodded, glancing back at the dancers as he led her away from the crowd.

They continued down two more blocks, then cut over three more. She was beginning to wonder if they would ever reach Back in the Day when Henry came to a stop. His brow was furrowed as he looked up at the facade of a brick building.

The door was propped open. The sign above it read MULVANEY'S IRISH PUB.

"What are we doing?" she asked.

He shook his head. "This should be it."

She returned her gaze to the sign. "The Irish pub?"

He pointed to a green awning. "Two sixty-one East Fourth Street."

She looked down the street, thinking maybe they were off by a few digits, but the only other businesses nearby were a nail parlor, an electronics shop, and a storefront advertising palm readings.

She took out her phone and pulled up the screenshot of Back in the Day's home page.

"Two sixty-one West Fourth . . ." She looked up at him. "*West* Fourth Street, not *East* Fourth Street. Henry, we're in the wrong place."

Twelve

Henry could only stare at her, dread blooming like an oil slick in his stomach. "You didn't say West Fourth Street. You just said Fourth Street. Or maybe you said East Fourth Street." He shook his head. "I don't know, but you definitely didn't say West Fourth Street."

She crossed her arms over her chest. "I'm sure I did. I read it right off the website."

"If you'd said West Fourth Street, we wouldn't be on East Fourth right now."

"So, this is my fault?" she asked, bright spots of pink appearing on her cheeks.

"I didn't say that."

"You implied it," she said.

"I'm sorry," he said. "I didn't mean to."

She turned around and put her hands on top of her head. "I knew this would happen. I knew it!"

"If you knew it would happen, why didn't you say something before we got on the subway in the first place?" he asked.

"You said you were sure!"

He sensed they were moving into dangerous territory. He had, after all, said he was sure.

"Listen, we ended up at the wrong place. It's not that big of a deal. I'll put the right address into my phone while we're aboveground. That way, if we have to get back on the subway we'll know for sure where we're going."

"I'll do it," she said, pulling out her phone.

"Two sixty-one West Fourth Street, right?" he asked, clicking past the text notifications from his mom. Violet could look it up if she wanted but he wasn't going to stand there like an idiot who couldn't even use the maps function on his phone.

"Yes. West Fourth Street. But I got it," she said. "It's in the West Village. We're in the East Village right now."

He wasn't sure he'd ever heard her sound so angry and accusatory. They'd had minor arguments, like the time she thought he'd been flirting with Nancy Kapoor at the Spring Fling and the time he'd suggested Violet have a heart-to-heart with her dad about giving them more space to be alone.

This felt different. Like there was another argument—one he wasn't really part of—running underneath the one he thought they were having.

"We have to get back on the subway at Bleecker Street," she said.

"I see it," he said, following the map on his own phone.

He hurried to catch up with her as she headed for the intersection. He wasn't going to follow her like a puppy just because she was mad. It wasn't like he didn't already feel bad. He couldn't even remember what she'd said back at the Bowling Green station, but he was fairly sure he'd used the address she'd given him when he'd chosen a subway. Now he felt embarrassed and stupid, the very last thing he wanted to be in Violet's eyes.

He kept pace with her as they crossed the street. The bustle of the city that had seemed exciting before their fight was now just a distraction. There was no way he could really talk to Violet while they wove their way through other pedestrians on their way to the subway station, the noise nearly deafening as they passed an orange-vested construction worker demolishing concrete with a jackhammer.

He tried in vain to remember their conversation back at the Bowling Green station, then put it out of his mind. It didn't matter anyway. Rehashing their argument wasn't going to make it better. The only thing that would do that was getting to Back in the Day and getting the notebook. Once she had it in her hands, they could enjoy the rest of the day together and this would all be a funny story to tell their friends—once they were un-grounded, that is.

He stuffed his hands in his pockets and tried to pretend he believed that.

Thirteen

Violet was still angry when they got off the subway in the West Village, but now she knew she wasn't mad at Henry.

She was mad at herself.

She'd had a feeling they were getting on the wrong train even before they stepped through the turnstile at the Bowling Green station. The subway map had been right in front of her. No one had stopped her from figuring out where they were going. She had willingly given the decision to Henry, just like she had so many times before.

She was glad he didn't try to talk to her as they made their way across Washington Square Park. She owed him an apology—after all, he'd apologized for steering them to the wrong part of the city—but she wasn't quite ready to say the words. She tried instead to remember times when she'd made decisions rather than relying on Henry.

There were some, but if she was being honest with herself, they were few and far between. It was just easier to let Henry call the shots. She'd had an excuse in the beginning. Coming to Storybrooke from Camelot had been a shock. Everything was different: the food, the music, transportation, the way people talked. There were refrigerators and microwave ovens, motorized cars and television, computers and cell phones. She was overwhelmed and overstimulated for the first year she was there, her only refuge the long hours she spent riding Nicodemus. Henry had been a comfort, gently teaching her all the things she needed to know to function and survive in the modern world.

But she'd been in Storybrooke for years now. It was home. Big cities didn't overwhelm her as much as they excited her. She could have made the decision back at the first subway station. It was true that the map looked like a lot of nonsense at first, but she'd figured it out on her phone once they got to the East Village. If she'd given herself some time, if she'd forced herself to come up with the answer, she might have gotten them to the right place.

Then again, she might have steered them wrong, too, gotten them lost in a completely different way. But so what if she had? At least it would have been her decision and her mistake. They'd managed to get back on track from the East Village. They could have done the same thing from anywhere in the city. Making a wrong decision suddenly didn't seem nearly as bad as letting someone else make a wrong decision for you.

A gentle breeze touched her skin, lifting her hair ever so slightly, and the scent of fresh-cut grass broke through her thoughts. She shook off her musing and looked around.

Flowers blossomed alongside the walkway, and up ahead, a grand fountain sprayed water into the air, the famous Washington Square arch rising into the sky beyond it. Parents walked next to their children on bicycles and the city's dog owners were out in force, marching alongside their leashed charges. A kind of celebration was in the air, as if everyone was part of a big reunion after the long winter. Even the people in business attire walking purposefully past seemed a little more relaxed there.

She drew in a breath and tried to let go of her earlier frustration. Henry was still silent beside her, and while she was grateful he'd given her some space to gather her thoughts, she needed to make it right with him. He'd only been trying to help. It wasn't fair to punish him for making the decision she hadn't wanted to make.

She reached for his hand as they approached the fountain and led him to the low wall that ran around the water.

"Let's stop for a minute," she said, pulling him down next to her on the wall.

"Shouldn't we hurry?" he asked. "We've already lost a lot of time."

"We can afford a couple minutes, I think."

He nodded and looked down at the flowers sprinkled across the skirt of her dress.

"I'm sorry, Henry. I shouldn't have gotten so angry."

"It's okay," he said.

She shook her head and looked up into his eyes. "No, it's not. You were right; I should have said something if I had doubts. You were willing to lead the way and I'm grateful for that. I was just frustrated that we'd ended up in the wrong place."

"I understand," he said. "I'm sorry I got us on the wrong train. But there is a bright side, you know."

"What's that?" she asked.

He grinned. "It will make for a great story."

She laughed. "Next year when we're un-grounded, you mean?"

"That's exactly what I mean." He turned to face her, taking her other hand in his and looking into her eyes. "I hate it when we fight."

"Me too."

He bent his head and touched his lips gently to hers. For a moment there was no doubt, no fear, nothing but him and the soft stroke of his hand against her cheek.

"This is my favorite part about being in the city," he said.

She stood. "Then we better get moving before we both decide to stay here all day instead of getting my father's notebook."

"Good point," he said.

They held hands as they continued through the park. Everything suddenly felt right with the world, the colors brighter, the birds louder, Henry's hand strong around hers. Her earlier concerns seemed minor. She'd been overanalyzing, caught up in her frustration about the time they'd lost going to the East Village.

They exited the park and continued through the city. The neighborhood was quiet and leafy, with more pedestrians and fewer cars than there had been in the East Village. They passed a little garden with a memorial to something called Stonewall. The shade beckoned, iron benches sitting under giant trees, coral tiger lilies blossoming along the path. It looked like a lovely way to pass the time if only they had time to spare.

"This is it," Henry said, looking from his phone to a sign that read W 4 ST.

Violet's heart lifted. They were almost there. She would finally have her father's notebook in her hands. Then maybe she and Henry could actually enjoy their remaining time together instead of arguing over decisions and directions.

She looked up at the numbers on the storefronts as they started down the street. There was a restaurant near the corner, followed by a boutique with vibrant dresses in the window and what looked like a doorway to a home or apartment. The numbers were descending. She kept track of them as they walked, getting closer to 261.

267 . . . 265 . . . 263 . . . 261.

She lowered her eyes to the storefront, her mind not quite registering what she was seeing. "This can't be right," she said.

Henry walked up to the giant window and the words painted on the glass. "'Closed for business,'" he read. "'Thank you for your patronage.'" He turned to look at her. "I'm so sorry, Violet."

Fourteen

"Closed for business?" Violet repeated. "That's it? Just . . . closed for business?"

"Maybe there's something about it online," Henry said, pulling out his phone as desperation began to set in. This was not how the mission to get Sir Morgan's notebook—or his day with Violet—was supposed to go.

A singsongy voice erupted to his left and he looked over to see a bedraggled elderly man sitting with his back against the brick building. He wore a tweed coat that was full of holes, his shoes highly shined. A black hat sat next to him on the pavement.

"Whitney comes to Fourth Street, to bring Mildred and Emmett a morning treat," he sang.

Henry sighed and turned his attention back to his phone. There was a new message from his mom.

YOU ARE IN SO MUCH TROUBLE, KID.

Didn't he know it.

He hesitated over the text, knowing he should reply, then swiped past it to his browser. She didn't sound totally freaked, at least. It was something.

Besides, Violet needed him. He'd already let her down with the subway out of the Bowling Green station and he couldn't help feeling like there might be more at stake than her father's notebook.

He clicked around Back in the Day's website, searching for some kind of announcement about their plans to close.

"Then it's on to Tiffany's shiny rings," the man on the sidewalk continued singing, *"until the next day when she brings more delicious things."*

Henry sighed and looked up at him. "Do you mind?"

"Henry!" Violet scolded.

"I'm sorry," he murmured as he clicked through the antiques shop's website. "It's distracting."

"That's no excuse to be rude," she said.

He looked up. Violet was always kind, always thinking of others. It was one of the things he loved about her. "You're right." He looked at the man. "I'm sorry."

The man didn't seem bothered as he launched into another round. *"Whitney comes to Fourth Street, to bring Mildred and Emmett a morning treat. . . ."*

"Right," Henry said, returning his attention to his phone. When he'd gone through Back in the Day's web pages twice, he looked at Violet. "There's nothing there. Not a word about them closing."

"It doesn't make sense." Despair had crept into her voice. "How can they just close without any kind of warning?"

Henry looked at the window. "They warned their local customers at least. They must have forgotten to update the website."

He walked to the glass and put his hands around his face to block out the sun while he peered into the dim recesses of the store. He needed to buy some time, figure out what was next. Violet was counting on him.

"What do you see?" she asked.

"Nothing much," he said, scanning the space. "It looks like they might have closed a while ago. There's a ladder, plus a paint can and a tarp. I wonder if the owner of the building is painting for a new tenant."

He lowered his hands and turned to face her.

"What do we do now?" she asked.

He desperately searched his mind for an answer. "I don't know."

He'd never hated saying those words more.

Fifteen

"I can't believe this," Violet said, despair threatening to overwhelm her. "Everything we've done has been for nothing. Leaving the others . . . missing the field trip . . . worrying your mom . . . it was all just a huge waste of time."

There was no point to her venting, but she couldn't seem to stop the words from spilling out of her mouth. She hadn't realized how important getting the notebook was to her until the moment it truly became out of reach. She saw her father's sagging shoulders, the way he paced the house in Storybrooke like he was trying to find his way back to his past. The notebook would have made it better. It would have given him back a piece of himself that he thought he'd lost a long time ago.

And now there was no way for her to find it.

Unless . . .

She took out her phone.

"What are you doing?" Henry asked.

"What I should have done in the first place—calling the number on the website."

She waited as the phone rang then listened as a breathy voice erupted on the other end.

"Hello, you've reached Mildred Appleby, owner of Back in the Day antiques. I'm not available to take your call, but if you leave a brief message, I'll get back to you as soon as possible. Thank you for calling Back in the Day!"

Violet waited for the beep to leave a message.

"Hello, my name is Violet Morgan and I'm interested in a piece you have listed on your website. I'm only in the city today, so if you could call me back as soon as possible, I'd appreciate it."

She left her number and disconnected the call.

Something was teasing her mind, but she couldn't quite put her finger on it.

"Whitney comes to Fourth Street, to bring Mildred and Emmett a morning treat," the man on the sidewalk sang. She turned to look at him as he continued. *"Then it's on to Tiffany's shiny rings, until the next day when she brings more delicious things."*

"Why don't we ask around?" Henry asked. "We could make our way down the block, ask the other store owners if—"

"Shhh!" Violet said.

"Shhhh?"

"Sorry." She'd never shushed him before. "I just need to listen."

The man on the sidewalk launched into another round of the rhyme. She walked toward him with Henry on her heels.

"No offense, but I really don't think we have time for another verse of whatever this guy is singing," Henry said.

"He said Mildred," Violet said. "That's the name of

the woman who left the outgoing message for the store's voice mail. I think his rhyme means something!"

"Define 'something,'" Henry said.

The man continued as if she and Henry weren't at that very moment engaged in a debate about the merit of his song. *"Whitney comes to Fourth Street, to bring Mildred and Emmett a morning treat."*

"I think he's trying to tell us something about the antiques store," Violet said.

She lowered herself to the pavement and smiled at him. "Hello," she said. "I like your song. Are you Emmett?"

The man grinned, his teeth surprisingly white and straight. *"Then it's on to Tiffany's shiny rings, until the next day when she brings more delicious things."*

"Is Whitney your friend?" she asked.

"Okay," Henry said, clearly exasperated, "why don't you have a chat with our friend here, and I'll go talk to the other store owners on the block."

She looked up at him. "I'm telling you, this is some kind of message."

"Whitney comes to Fourth Street . . ."

Violet stood and brushed off her dress, the words ringing in her mind. There was something about them, something too intentional to be pure imagination. She'd regretted ignoring her instinct at the Bowling Green station. She wasn't going to make the same mistake this time.

"Let's just go with this for a minute," she said.

Henry sighed. "If you say so."

"If Whitney is a real person, he's saying she comes to the store with some kind of treat for the owner or manager and someone named Emmett. What if it's him? What if he's Emmett, and Whitney brings something for him and Mildred every morning?" She paced the sidewalk. "Bagels? Pastries?"

"I'm not sure the difference between bagels and pastries is going to crack the code," Henry said.

Violet suppressed her annoyance. She always went along with Henry. She'd think this once he could give her the benefit of the doubt.

Henry bent down to the man on the sidewalk. "Is your name Emmett? Does Whitney bring you breakfast?"

"*Whitney comes to Fourth Street . . .*"

"Okay, then." Henry straightened. "This isn't working."

"If Mildred owns or manages the store, Whitney must be some kind of friend, which means if we can find Whitney . . ." Violet listened as the man on the sidewalk started the second verse of the rhyme. "Then it's on to Tiffany's shiny rings, until the next day when she brings more delicious things," she murmured along with him.

"Is Tiffany another friend maybe?" Henry asked.

"Maybe?" At least he was helping instead of complaining.

Tiffany's shiny rings . . .

"A friend who wears a lot of jewelry . . ." Violet tried it out. "A friend who sells jewelry . . ." And then, all at once, it was there. She tugged on Henry's arm. "Tiffany! The jewelry store!"

"Um . . . what jewelry store?" Henry asked.

"Tiffany!" she said. "Only the most famous jewelry store in New York City!"

"Never heard of it."

She laughed and wrapped her arms around him, jubilant with the possibility of tracking down the owner of the antiques store. "It's a New York City icon!" She pulled back to look at him. "What if this woman—"

"Whitney," he said.

"Right. What if Whitney works at Tiffany? What if she brings Mildred—and Emmett here—breakfast on her way to work every day? If she does, she might be able to connect us to Mildred. We might still be able to buy the notebook!"

"It's kind of a long shot." He looked at his phone. "Plus, it's almost two, which means we only have a couple hours before we have to meet everyone at Chelsea Piers."

She took a deep breath. "I know, but it's worth looking into, right? And if I'm wrong, we'll call it a day."

He rubbed a hand over his face, something he did when he was only going along with something to make her happy. She didn't care. He didn't have to like it; he just had to agree to it.

"I need to do this," she said. "I need to know I've done everything possible to get the notebook for my father."

"Okay," he said.

She turned to the man on the sidewalk and bent to take his hands in hers. "Thank you, Emmett," she said. "Thank you so much. I'll tell Whitney you said hello."

He was making his way through the rhyme again as they hurried for the corner.

Sixteen

Henry tried to keep his spirits up as they entered the subway and headed uptown. The system seemed less mysterious now that they'd used it to wander the city, but they were still careful to get directions before they went underground. That wasn't a lesson he wanted to learn twice.

Violet's mood had improved considerably since their meeting with the man on the sidewalk outside Back in the Day's former storefront. Henry had his doubts; the guy hadn't seemed like he was all there. Still, it wasn't like Henry had a better idea than heading to Tiffany in search of a woman named Whitney. It would probably be a dead end, but it bought him some time to come up with a plan B. Never mind that he wasn't entirely sure there *was* a plan B. Violet had agreed to give up if the trip to Tiffany didn't pan out, and while he wasn't looking forward to her disappointment, at least they'd know they'd done everything possible to find her father's notebook. Maybe then they could rejoin the group and enjoy the rest of the field trip—after the inevitable lecture by Emma, of course.

To say the day hadn't gone as planned was an understatement. In all his imaginings, he'd never expected so many missteps, so many unforeseen obstacles. The harried, stressful day they'd shared so far was a far cry from the romantic adventure through New York City he'd envisioned. More than that, Violet herself seemed unusually tense. He wanted to believe it was the situation—the frustration and disappointment over all the roadblocks they'd hit along the way coupled with being in a strange city.

But that didn't ring entirely true. It wasn't anything she'd said but a distance that had opened between them. At first it had felt like a minor fracture, but as the day wore on, it was beginning to feel more like an impassable canyon, even when she went through the motions of holding his hand and kissing him.

He considered talking to her about it as they exited the subway near Central Park. His moms always said communication was the most important thing in a relationship. Emma and Killian had their share of disagreements, but they managed to resolve them. Regina always told him it was natural to disagree with the person you loved, since loving someone didn't mean you felt exactly the same about everything.

He'd certainly seen enough evidence of it in the lives of the people around him. He couldn't even remember all the times his family and friends in Storybrooke had been angry with each other—even seeming to hate each other sometimes—only to come back together in the end.

He and Violet loved each other. He would talk to her

when he had the chance and they would clear the air, work everything out.

He took her hand and looked around, marveling at Central Park. It took his breath away to see the giant park, seemingly dropped into the city by some unseen hand. It was almost magical—the lush greenery standing in stark contrast to the glinting steel and glass of the buildings, which kissed the sky like an assortment of modern castles.

"This path should take us to Fifth Avenue," he said, taking a walkway that forked to the right after glancing at the map on his phone.

"I can't believe this is all here," Violet said, looking around in wonder.

"You've never seen the park?" Henry asked.

"Not in person," she said. "I didn't realize it was so big."

"Even bigger than it looks from here," he said. He wished they had time to explore. He would've loved to walk with Violet to the lake where they could rent a paddleboat. He would've taken her to see the *Alice in*

Wonderland statue where Alice sat atop her giant mushroom, the Mad Hatter and the White Rabbit at her feet. They would've followed it all up with the carousel, where they would've listened to the old-fashioned music astride brightly colored mounts. Most of all, he wished he could've taken Violet on a carriage ride through the park. There was nothing more romantic, and he felt sure the new tension between them would've dissipated within the cozy confines of one of the park's horse-drawn carriages.

"How far is it?" Violet asked.

The question brought him back to the present. Maybe if they found the notebook—or discovered that it was a lost cause—quickly enough, they would have time for a carriage ride before they rejoined the group.

Henry looked at his phone. "Not far. This path should take us back to the city, near Lexington."

They turned right on the path and continued past a child carrying a red balloon, an elderly woman walking an elaborately shorn poodle, and a man in a suit talking animatedly on his phone.

The sounds of the city became louder as they came to the edge of the park. They reached the sidewalk and Henry's stomach grumbled as the scent of cooking meat hit his nostrils.

He turned to Violet. "Hey, are you hungry?"

She smiled. "Starving."

"Come on."

He followed the scent to a cart parked near the curb. Hot dogs sizzled as they rotated between metal rollers, and containers held relish and onions, peppers and sauerkraut, even jalapeños. Henry could smell them through the sneeze guard that had been erected around the edges of the cart.

He stepped up and ordered two hot dogs and two sodas. The man handed Henry his plain hot dog and then loaded Violet's with some of everything. Violet liked to try new food, and Henry couldn't help smiling at the look of excitement on her face as the man behind the cart handed her the paper container filled with her feast.

"Let's find a place to sit," Henry said.

He led her to an empty bench at the edge of the park and they took a seat. Violet groaned as she bit into the hot dog, closing her eyes as the full force of the flavors hit her mouth. She'd only been chewing for a few seconds when her eyes flew open and she reached for her soda.

"It's so spicy," she said with a gasp.

Henry laughed. "I told you the jalapeños were hot."

"Hot and delicious," she said, taking another bite.

Henry took out his phone to see how close they were to Tiffany & Co. A new text had come through while they'd been in the park, this one from Killian.

SERIOUSLY NOT COOL, MATE. YOUR MOM IS WORRIED.

Somehow the text from Killian made him feel worse than the ones from his mom. Emma prided herself on being cool under pressure. She hadn't seemed panicked in her texts to Henry, but she must have been more worried than she was letting on.

He opened the text window for his mom and started typing.

I'M SORRY. WE'RE OKAY. I PROMISED VIOLET I'D HELP HER WITH AN ERRAND. WE'LL MEET UP WITH YOU FOR BOWLING.

He sent the text and slipped his phone back into his pocket. He didn't want to argue with his mom. Violet needed him more than ever and he wasn't about to let her down. He needed to prove she could count on him. He was going to help her see the mission through to the end.

"That was amazing!" Violet said, wiping her mouth with one of the napkins they'd grabbed from the cart.

Henry smiled. "Do you want another one?"

She burped a little, then laughed. "That probably isn't a good idea. Besides, we have to get to Tiffany."

"True." Henry stood and dropped their trash in a nearby receptacle, then took out his phone to orient them toward the jewelry store. "Let's go."

They crossed the street and started down Fifth Avenue.

Violet's face lit up. "I don't think we're in Kansas anymore, Toto."

"You aren't kidding," Henry said, taking in the giant Gucci sign looming over the pristine street.

It wasn't the East or West Village, that was for

sure. Here everything sparkled as if it had been freshly scrubbed and then polished to a high shine. Most of the cars on the street were taxis, limousines, or black cars with darkened windows. Logos for the most famous brands in the world sparkled above: Chanel and Prada, Cartier and Saks, Rolex and even Harry Winston, who Regina said had the best jewelry every year when she watched the Oscars.

They headed toward the blue dot on his maps app, stopping every so often to look through the big glass storefronts. It wasn't that Henry wanted any of the stuff on display; it was just all so new. So . . . shiny.

"I think that's it!" Violet said.

He followed her pointed finger to a glass window adorned with a shade of blue almost the exact color of a robin's egg.

"How do you know?" he asked.

She grinned and took his hand. "Trust me."

Seventeen

Violet's stomach fluttered with nervousness and excitement as they headed for the big gold letters spelling out TIFFANY & CO. If she was right about the man outside Back in the Day's former storefront, they might be one step closer to finding her father's notebook.

If she was wrong, the search would be over.

She hesitated in front of one of the big windows. Diamonds winked from the other side of the glass and elegant blue boxes were displayed like art under the lights.

"What's wrong?" Henry asked.

"Nothing," she said. "It's just . . ."

"What?"

"What if I was wrong? What if the man back in the West Village was loopy and Whitney has nothing at all to do with Back in the Day?"

"Then we'll have to figure something else out," Henry said. "And hey, leaving the city without the notebook doesn't mean you'll never find it again. Once we're back in Storybrooke, we can always try tracking the owner of the store through old business listings or something. There has to be a way to find her with more time than we have today. Plus, you left a message. Someone might still call you back."

Violet looked down at her shoes and nodded. It was sweet of Henry to try to make her feel better, but she had a feeling if they left the city without the notebook she would never find it again.

"I'm sure you're right." There was no point making him feel bad when he was just trying to help. "Thanks."

He gave her a quick hug. "You're welcome. Now let's go find Whitney of the delicious treats."

Violet laughed a little and opened the door to the store.

She was barely across the threshold when she came to a stop, overcome with awe. She'd seen *Breakfast at Tiffany's* more than once, but the store was so much grander in person than it had seemed on television.

The space was huge, the double-height ceilings studded with small lights that looked like stars. The front of the store was situated with several glass cases, each of them showcasing an array of precious jewels, gold, and silver, all of it sparkling like sunshine on water.

Henry pulled her gently to the side as someone came in through the doors behind them.

"No offense," he said, "but we should probably do something. That security guard looks like he thinks we're going to rob the place or something."

Violet followed his gaze to a big man in a perfectly tailored suit. "How do you know he's a security guard?" Violet asked.

"He's not just window-shopping, standing like that," Henry said.

She saw his point. The man's legs were slightly spread, arms crossed in front of his body as he stared at them. His gaze was like a laser beam on her face. It was hard to imagine him seeing her and Henry as any kind of threat, but she started walking around the first display anyway in an effort to show him they meant no harm.

"How do you want to handle this?" Henry asked as she hesitated over an array of sapphires: a necklace heavy with stones, earrings that dripped blue fire, a bracelet that somehow managed to look both fierce and delicate with its alternating diamonds and sapphires.

"How may I help you?"

Violet looked up into the brown eyes of a middle-aged man in a suit. "I'm looking for a friend. A friend named Whitney. I think she works here."

The words tumbled out of her mouth before she could stop them. She didn't know whether to be embarrassed by her boldness or impressed with herself.

"A friend named Whitney?" the man repeated.

Violet took a deep breath. She was in it now. There was nothing to do but commit and see where it led them.

"That's right."

"Do you know what department she works in?" the man asked.

He didn't seem at all suspicious, and why should he? They were two teenagers looking for someone. Nothing more and nothing less.

"I'm sorry, I don't," she said.

"I see." The man rubbed his smoothly shaven jaw. "Please wait one moment."

"Thank you."

He turned away and headed behind a bank of cabinets at the center of the display.

"Wow, you really went for it," Henry said.

Violet looked up at him. "Do you have a better idea?"

He shook his head. "Not at all. I was just surprised."

"Why?" The question came out sharper than she'd intended, but the idea of Henry being surprised by her assertiveness didn't sit well. Did he think she was weak? Incapable of making decisions or taking action without him?

He shrugged. "I just didn't expect it."

The man reappeared at the counter in front of them. "I'm told there is a Whitney Day upstairs in handbags. I don't know if it's your friend—and I don't know if she's working today—but she's the only Whitney employed at this location."

Violet pushed the implication of Henry's earlier statement to the back of her mind. She'd been right! The man on the sidewalk had been trying to tell them something. Maybe Whitney wouldn't be able to help them, but the fact that Violet had solved the riddle at all gave her a strange sense of satisfaction.

"Thank you so much," Violet said.

"You can take the escalator or the elevator," the man said.

They headed deeper into the store toward the escalators. Violet felt like she was floating as they rose slowly and smoothly toward the second floor, a glass half-wall decorated with gold trailing vines coming into view as they reached the top.

She was already rehearsing the question she would

have to ask to find her way to the handbag department when she saw the sign clearly marking that section of the store.

She felt giddy as she and Henry stepped over the threshold into a fantasy land of leather and suede, velvet and satin. Jewels shone from some of the bags, a constellation of brightness under the lights of the store. At the center of it all was a glass counter. Behind it, two women stood quietly talking.

Violet could only hope one of them was Whitney Day.

Eighteen

Henry had been a lot of weird places in his life, but none had felt as foreign as the store that now surrounded him. It was as quiet and hushed as a library, customers and employees alike seeming to drift a foot above the floor when they walked, their silence indicating a kind of reverence he didn't understand. Crystals dripped from the light fixtures and diamonds shimmered on everything from the necklaces and bracelets and rings downstairs to the fancy handbags on the walls of the second floor. It was like stepping into a jewelry box and having someone turn up the lights, then close the lid.

He let Violet lead the way toward the counter where two women stood talking quietly to each other. They turned toward Henry and Violet even before they reached the counter.

"Good afternoon." The woman who spoke was about Regina's age, with sleek red hair pulled into a knot at the back of her neck. "How can we help you?"

The question seemed directed at Violet, and for once Henry was more than happy to let her take over.

"I'm looking for someone named Whitney," Violet said. "I . . . I was told she might work here."

The second woman straightened, a look of confusion passing over her smooth unlined face. "My name is Whitney. Whitney Day."

She was younger than the first woman, maybe not much older than Violet, but where the other woman's hair sparkled like a copper penny under the lights, Whitney's was like a golden halo, swinging smooth and glossy around her shoulders. She wore a crisp blue suit with a white blouse. A simple gold chain with a small diamond at its center shimmered around her neck.

Violet bit her lower lip, clearly trying to summon the right words to explain their situation. Henry was getting ready to step in when she spoke.

"This is going to sound strange, but would you happen to know the antiques store Back in the Day?" she asked the young woman. "It's in the West Village on West Fourth Street."

A flash of surprise lit the woman's blue eyes. "That's my grandmother's store. . . . Is she all right?"

"Oh, yes!" Violet said, taking in a breath of air. "Of course! I'm so sorry to worry you."

Henry was still processing the woman's admission that she knew the owner of the antiques store. Violet had been right after all; the woman named Mildred was Whitney's grandmother.

"It's all right," Whitney said. "She recently closed the shop, but I thought maybe she'd forgotten something and had gone back."

"It's nothing like that." Violet glanced at the older woman. "I . . . I was hoping you might be able to help me."

"I'm going to check that new inventory in the back,"

the older woman said to Whitney. "Let me know if you need anything."

She stepped from the confines of the counter and disappeared through a small door at the back of the space. Whitney watched her go, then turned to Violet.

"I'd be happy to help if I can," Whitney said, "but like I said, my grandmother doesn't own the store anymore. The rent has gotten ridiculous in that part of the city. She just couldn't do it, and since most of her business is done online with private clients now . . ."

"I understand," Violet said. "That's how I found her, actually—on the internet."

"You know my grandmother?" Whitney asked.

"Oh, no. Not yet. But she had a notebook for sale that may have belonged to an ancestor of mine. I'm in the city just for today and had hoped to have a look at it," Violet said.

"Goodness!" Whitney said. "You must have been so surprised to find the store closed. I'm always on her to update the website, but she doesn't like dealing with it much." A shadow of sadness passed across her eyes. "In fact, I think she's going to miss talking to customers in person. That was always her favorite part."

"I was surprised," Violet admitted. "And worried. If the notebook is what I think it is, a member of my family would very much love to have it. I was hoping to make her an offer on it. I suppose I should have called first."

Whitney's smile was sympathetic. "It's hardly your fault when there was no closing notice online."

"I wonder . . ." Violet hesitated, then charged ahead. "Is there any way you can put us in touch with her?

Whitney tapped her fingers on the counter. "Can you hold on for a moment?"

"Of course," Violet said.

She turned to Henry with a shrug as Whitney walked to the other end of the counter area. She picked up a phone hidden behind the counter and turned her back to them.

"Do you think it will work?" Henry asked Violet.

"I don't know," Violet said. "I hope so."

Henry looked around. "This isn't like any jewelry store I've ever seen."

Violet laughed softly. "Me neither."

"How much do you think all this stuff costs?" Henry asked.

"More than I make in a year at the bookstore," Violet said.

It was hard to imagine spending that much money on something, but when he looked at the sparkle in Violet's eyes, it got easier. He could imagine her smile if he were to hand her a pretty necklace in one of the blue boxes tied with white ribbon he had seen some of the sales clerks downstairs presenting to their customers. Even something simple like the necklace worn by Whitney Day would be nice.

He looked up to see Whitney setting down the phone. She walked toward them with a smile. "My grandmother isn't answering her phone at the moment, but I think it will be okay for me to introduce you. She'll probably be happy for the company."

"Are you sure?" Violet asked. "I don't want to intrude,

but it would be wonderful if you really think it's okay."

"I'm sure," Whitney said. "I don't get off for another hour though. Can you wait?"

"We can wait," Violet said firmly.

Henry thought about the texts from his mom. He didn't love the idea of leaving her hanging, and if they waited for Whitney, they definitely weren't meeting up with the group in time for Chelsea Piers. They'd still be back at the hotel for the dinner cruise on the Hudson River, but their punishment was likely to be a lot more severe. On the other hand, it was more time with Violet—time he increasingly felt they needed, although he couldn't have said why.

He stayed quiet. In for a penny, in for a pound, as Regina always said.

"Great," Whitney said. "I'll meet you out front."

"Thank you again," Violet said. "I can't tell you how much I appreciate it."

"It's no problem at all," Whitney said. "It's a little exciting, really!"

She looked up, and Henry followed her gaze to a

fashionably dressed woman who had stepped over the threshold into the handbag department.

"See you in an hour," Violet whispered as they stepped away from the counter.

Henry caught the subtle whiff of perfume as they passed the woman on her way into the department. He couldn't help feeling like they'd been transported to another world as they made their way back down the escalator—and judging from the shine in Violet's eyes, it was one she liked more than he did.

Nineteen

"We have an hour to kill," Violet said when they were back outside the store. "Want to do some window-shopping?"

Henry shrugged. "Sure."

He didn't seem enthused.

"Is there something else you'd rather do?" she asked.

"Not really," he said. "Window-shopping is fine."

They started down the street, glancing through the glass at the fronts of some of the stores, pausing to look longer at others. The window displays were so lavish that Violet had to resist the urge to stop and stare at every one. There were beautiful dresses and perfectly tailored slacks, leather handbags that looked as soft as velvet, and shoes with ribbons and heels so high she couldn't fathom how anyone walked in them.

She'd never given much thought to her wardrobe. Emma had helped her pick suitable clothes when she'd first come to Storybrooke. The selection had seemed dizzying even at the small mall near town and she still felt perversely free in the sundresses and flat shoes that she'd come to favor.

Now she found herself feeling plain and dowdy. Everything in New York City was so sleek and modern. She suddenly had the urge to go in and try on the simple shifts, the silk drawstring pants with elastic at the ankles, the mauve velvet shoes with bows that tied behind the ankles.

But of course, she couldn't do that. Henry would think she was crazy. He'd already been more than accommodating on their chaotic mission to retrieve her father's notebook.

Still, as they continued around the block, she couldn't

help wondering what it would be like to be alone in the city, to have the freedom to go anywhere and do anything she pleased without a word to anyone. She could see herself, a new Violet, one who was fashionable and brave and knew the city like the back of her hand.

She glanced at Henry and felt a burst of remorse. Doing those things would mean leaving him behind, and he'd been so good to her. That counted for a lot, didn't it?

Her phone buzzed inside her bag and she removed it to find a text from Sadie.

MR. BLANKENSHIP IS LOSING IT. WHAT ARE YOU DOING?

Violet's stomach twisted into a knot. What *was* she doing? She was a good daughter, a good student, a rule follower. She and Henry needed to wrap up the search for her father's notebook right away and get to Chelsea Piers if they had any hope of redeeming themselves with Mr. Blankenship, to say nothing of Emma, Killian, and Mary Margaret.

They came to a fancy pen store called Montblanc, and Violet suggested they stop to look. It was more

Henry's speed and she pointed out a beautiful burgundy pen with a gold tip lying on a bed of satin.

"Wouldn't it be nice to work on The Book with such a lovely pen?" she asked.

"I don't need a fancy pen to work on The Book."

She turned to look at him, startled by the sharpness in his tone. "Are you angry with me, Henry?"

He sighed. "I just don't understand why you like all this stuff."

"All what stuff?"

He waved his hand around. "The fancy clothes and jewelry, the city, all of it."

"But you said you love the city."

Where was this coming from?

"I like visiting the city," he said. "You seem to love it a bit more than I do."

"Why is it bad if we like different things?" she asked.

"I don't know," he said. "It's not, I guess."

"Then why are you acting this way?"

"Acting what way?"

"Angry and annoyed. Maybe it's because . . . Never mind. " She turned away and looked into the window of the store, the words she wanted to say on the tip of her tongue.

"No, go ahead," he said. "Say what you want to say."

"It's like you were mad that I was right about Whitney Day, and now you're mad that I happen to like the city, even though I thought that was the point of today. I thought we were *supposed* to like the city, that we were supposed to enjoy being here together."

"We are." He wasn't looking at her, and his voice sounded funny.

"Then what's going on?"

"It feels like it's more than you liking the city," he said.

"More?"

He looked straight ahead, his reflection staring back at her from the store window, the pen gleaming on its satin bed like a precious jewel. "It just seems like things have been weird between us, that's all," he said.

"Weird how?" she asked.

But she already knew what he meant; things *had* been weird between them. She just needed time to figure out why.

At first, she had thought it was being in the city, the pressure of having to give Emma and Killian the slip, the frustration of getting lost and losing the trail of the notebook, the ticking clock on the time they had left.

Now she wasn't so sure. Being in the city made everything look different. Maybe she'd always been too willing to let Henry lead the way. Maybe it was like a bad habit, something that had started when she was new to Storybrooke. Maybe she'd just gotten used to it.

It was easier in Storybrooke. There weren't so many decisions to make there, so many opportunities for them to disagree. They met outside the library every morning at school and sat at the same table at lunch every day. They had predetermined meeting places between classes. They went to Granny's Diner after school, where Henry got mozzarella sticks and she ordered French fries. Then they walked the same way home, kissing goodbye on the corner before they were in view of her house. He dropped her off before heading to one of his moms' houses, and they spent the evening texting while they did homework.

What was there to argue about?

"I guess it just feels like you're . . . pulling away a little," he finally said.

"Because I'm making decisions on my own? Because I can sometimes take care of myself?" She was as surprised by the vehemence in her voice as she was by the anger that accompanied it.

He turned to look at her. "That's a mean thing to say, Violet."

She started walking away from him, crossing her arms in front of her chest as she made her way down the street. It was reflexive. She didn't know what to do with all the feelings pushing their way through her chest and up into her throat.

"You're just going to walk away?" Henry asked, catching up to her. "You're not even going to talk to me now?"

"What do you want me to say, Henry? We both

agree things have been weird today. To be honest, I think maybe they've been weird for a while and we just didn't know it."

He took her hand to stop her forward motion. "What are you talking about?"

She shook her head, tears stinging her eyes. "I don't know. I don't know what's happening, but we need to get back. Whitney will be off work soon and she might not wait if we're not there."

"Don't you think we should talk about this?" Henry asked.

"Yes," she said. "I actually do think we should talk about it, but not right now."

He sighed, dropping her hand. "All right. Whatever you say."

They made their way back around the block in silence. A new kind of sadness had opened up in Violet's heart. When she thought about it, she realized it was the melancholy of loss.

Which didn't make any sense at all.

Twenty

Henry had to force a smile onto his face when Whitney stepped out of the store. After a quick introduction—he and Violet had never actually introduced themselves—they started down the street.

It was a relief to hear Whitney and Violet talking to each other about the city, Whitney's job at Tiffany, and her apartment in Chelsea. No one expected him to talk, which was good, because he wasn't sure he would have been able to put together a coherent statement with all the thoughts running through his head. He was still thinking about his conversation with Violet.

What had she meant when she'd said things had been weird for a while? They were happy together. At least, he'd thought they were. Being with Violet was like living in a perfect sunny day every day of the week. He knew exactly what to expect, and it was always as wonderful as he'd thought it would be.

Had it all been an illusion? Had Violet really been unhappy all that time? Was it his fault?

He searched his mind for answers to his questions, backtracking to all the ways he might have screwed up. There had been the big fight after the Spring Fling, but he'd apologized for flirting with Nancy (he hadn't thought he was flirting) and everything had seemed fine afterward. There was the occasional conflict over their limited time alone and her father's insistence on keeping track of Violet every second of every day, but that was no big deal. Violet had been just as frustrated as Henry had been.

Other than those things, there had been no sign of trouble, and yet their argument on the street didn't have the feel of a passing rain cloud—more like a thunderstorm whose electricity had been building in the air for a long time.

He worried as he trailed Whitney and Violet to the subway. It was strangely reassuring to be with Whitney, who spoke breezily as they made their way down the steps and through the turnstiles of the station without looking even once at her phone or the map on the station wall. After all the missteps of the day, it was a relief to be in someone else's capable hands, although he wouldn't have wanted Violet to know it.

"And what about you, Henry?" Whitney asked.

"What about me?" Henry repeated.

She smiled. "What are your plans after high school?"

"Oh . . . I don't know, actually. I'm still figuring it out." He'd never felt overly self-conscious about not having plans—they had a whole year before graduation—but now he felt lame and unambitious.

"Good for you. It's best to make sure you know what *you* want rather than doing what everyone else thinks you should do," Whitney said.

Henry managed a smile. "That's what I figure."

"Anyway, you have lots of time," Whitney said as she leaned forward to look for the train. "They always make it seem like you don't, but you do. I'm sure you'll figure it out."

He was saved from having to reply by a screeching sound from the tunnel. A moment later, the train barreled into the station amid a gust of hot, dry wind. They waited as a crowd exited the train, then stepped onto it right before the doors closed. Twenty minutes later, they were back aboveground and making their way down a narrow street, the spire of the Empire State Building piercing the sky in the distance.

Like all the neighborhoods they'd visited so far, SoHo had a personality all its own. The East Village had been a little retro, but obviously expensive. The West Village had been quainter—but still expensive. And of course, there was Fifth Avenue, its riches and excess like the glossy covers of the high-fashion magazines Regina always got in the mail but never seemed to read.

SoHo was a slice of old New York, its streets still

lined with faded cobblestone. The apartment buildings and row houses were lined up like statues, and fire escapes rose like sculptural scaffolding from their facades. They passed a brick building adorned with a stylized graffiti version of Alice falling down the rabbit hole.

There were no trees, but the neighborhood still felt warm and homey. Henry could picture it the way it must have been a hundred years earlier, neighbors shouting across the street to each other, their laundry waving like signal flags between the buildings.

His phone buzzed in his pocket and he removed it to find a text not from Emma or Killian, but from his grandmother.

THIS IS UNACCEPTABLE, HENRY. CALL YOUR MOTHER. NOW.

A wave of nausea rolled through him. The only thing worse than knowing his mom was worried was knowing he would have to face his grandmother's wrath. Mary Margaret might bake the best cookies in Storybrooke, but she had a way of making even his grandfather shake in his boots when she was angry.

He hoped they would be quick at Mildred's house. They had less than an hour before their window closed to meet up with everyone at Chelsea Piers.

"It's right up here," Whitney said, removing a set of keys from her handbag. "Gran still hasn't called me back, so I can't promise we'll catch her, but we can certainly try."

"We appreciate your help so much," Violet said as they approached a yellow brick building with a burnished wood door. "Don't we, Henry?"

"Definitely," Henry said.

What was wrong with him? He needed to get it together. So he and Violet had a fight. So what? They would talk later and he would smooth everything over.

Everything would be fine.

He said it again in his head, just to reassure himself. *Everything will be fine.*

Twenty-One

Violet watched as Whitney slipped her key in the lock and opened the door. They followed her into a tiled foyer flanked by two large plants.

"It's a walk-up," Whitney said. "Gran's on the third floor. I hope you don't mind."

"Not at all," Violet said.

She spoke quickly, guessing that Henry was still sulking. He hadn't said two words to her since their fight on the street. She was annoyed that he was being child-ish, but she didn't want to draw attention to that fact with Whitney.

They started up the stairs, continuing past the second floor. When they got to the third floor, Violet saw there were four doors clustered around the landing. Whitney headed for the one marked with the number twelve in shiny brass.

"I'm going to knock before I use my key," Whitney explained, raising her hand to the door.

She knocked softly. Violet held her breath. This was it. If Whitney's grandmother wasn't home, Violet would have to put off her search for her father's notebook. Maybe she could be in touch with the woman named Mildred over the phone once she got back to Storybrooke, but there was no way she and Henry would be able to get away from the field trip again.

Whitney knocked again. "Are you in there, Gran? It's me, Whitney."

Her voice was met with silence. She was lifting an old-fashioned key to the lock when the door flew open. The woman standing on the other side of the threshold was small, with wild red hair and porcelain skin so pale it was almost translucent.

"My goodness, Whitney, I told you to use your—"

She stopped mid-sentence when she spotted Violet and Henry.

"I tried calling, Gran, but you didn't answer your phone. This is Violet Morgan. She was interested in one of your pieces and didn't realize you had closed the store. This is her friend Henry. They came all the way from Maine." Having introduced Violet and Henry, Whitney looked at her grandmother. "This is my grandmother Mildred Appleby."

"It's nice to meet you." Violet held out her hand and was relieved when Henry followed suit. At least he hadn't lost sight of his manners.

"I suppose I should have put something on the internet about the closing after all," Mildred said as she shook their hands.

Whitney laughed. "I tried to tell you. Now are you going to invite us in or are we going to continue this in the hall?"

The woman stepped back and opened the door wider. "Of course. Come in." They stepped over the threshold as she continued, "I'm sorry I didn't answer the phone. I was cataloguing those old postcards I got in last week."

"It's okay, Gran," Whitney said.

They followed Mildred into a small living room lined with shelves. The place had an air of ordered chaos with knickknacks and books lining the shelves and a series of small tables scattered around the room. Violet wouldn't have been surprised if Mildred could produce even the smallest of items from the clutter without a second thought.

"Please make yourselves comfortable," Mildred said, picking up a stack of sheet music from one end of the couch and moving a framed abstract print from the other. "Would you like some tea?"

Violet thought about the text from Sadie: *Mr. Blankenship is losing it. What are you doing?*

"No, thank you," she said. "We can't stay long."

Mildred sat on a chair across from the sofa. It was upholstered with what looked like a rug, and stuffing was coming out in all directions, but it looked right at home in the messy warmth of the apartment.

"All right, what can I help you with, my dear?" she asked.

Violet pulled out her phone and found the screenshot of the notebook she'd taken from the internet. This was it. The notebook was somewhere in this very apartment and she was about to find out how much it would cost to return it to her father.

"It's this notebook," she said, handing over the phone. "I think it may have belonged to an ancestor of mine."

Mildred took off her eyeglasses and brought the phone closer to her face. "Oh, my. . . ."

The note of alarm in her voice prompted an answering call of concern within Violet.

"What is it?" she asked. She felt like a fist was squeezing her heart at the stricken expression on Mildred's face.

"I don't know quite how to say this," Mildred started, handing the phone back to Violet.

"Don't you recognize it?" Violet asked, desperation growing inside her. "It's on your website."

"I certainly do recognize it," she said. "But I'm afraid I sold it three days ago."

Twenty-Two

Henry couldn't say anything for a long moment. He was still processing Mildred Appleby's words and their implication. Violet had been right; they'd come all this way for nothing. They'd abandoned the group at Ellis Island and worried his mom for nothing. Maybe they'd even fought and gotten angry with each other for nothing.

"But it's still on the website . . ." he finally said. It sounded lame, but it was the only thing that came to mind. If the notebook had been sold, why was it still listed as available?

Mildred lifted a hand to her neck. She was clearly distressed. "Oh, my. . . . Whitney's always telling me I need to update the website. I'm afraid I've never been very good about it. I get so distracted with the inventory, and customers usually call or email to inquire about pricing—not that this is your fault," she added quickly, shaking her head. "No, this is my responsibility. I'm so very sorry."

Henry glanced at Violet, her face pale and stricken next to him. He reached for her hand but she quickly pulled it away. He tried not to feel stung. She couldn't possibly blame him for the fact that the notebook was gone, could she? It was sold days ago. None of their missteps had changed anything.

Still, he couldn't help feeling ashamed of his earlier selfishness. After they'd realized Back in the Day was closed, he'd wanted nothing more than to call it quits. He'd been anticipating that the moment they arrived at Tiffany they'd discover the man on the sidewalk had been rambling, not delivering some kind of message.

He'd been more than happy to call the mission to get Sir Morgan's notebook a failure if it meant he and Violet could return their focus to enjoying the day together. Now he wondered if the notebook was more than a means to spend time with Violet, if maybe it was the only way to ease the tension between them, to make their relationship the way it had been before they came to the city.

Getting the notebook suddenly felt more urgent than ever.

"I think I'll get Violet a drink of water," Whitney said, standing. "Can I get you anything, Henry?"

"No, thank you."

She stepped into the kitchen and Henry heard the water running in the sink. She returned a moment later with a glass and handed it to Violet.

"What about the buyer?" Violet asked after she'd taken a drink. Her voice was surprisingly forceful. Henry didn't recognize the glint in her eyes.

"The buyer?" Mildred repeated.

"The buyer of the notebook," Violet said. "Is he or she here in the city?"

Mildred's hand went to her neck again. "Well, yes. . . . I do believe he had an office here, but—"

"Perhaps you could give us his contact information," Violet suggested. "Maybe he'd like to resell it."

"Oh, I couldn't!" Mildred said. "It would be highly irregular."

Violet set the glass down on Mildred's coffee table and took a deep breath. "I wouldn't ask if I didn't think it might benefit him."

Mildred looked confused. "Benefit him?"

"Well," Violet said, "I assume you sometimes sell to other dealers who then turn around, mark up the price, and resell a piece to someone else."

"Yes, of course," Mildred said. "I do quite a lot of business that way."

"If I contacted the buyer of the notebook and offered him more than he paid, he would make a profit in only three days. He wouldn't even have to look for a buyer.

It seems to me you might actually be doing him a favor," Violet said.

Henry could hardly believe this was Violet—his Violet—negotiating with Mildred Appleby. Violet sounded so sure of herself, not at all shy or hesitant the way she often did in Storybrooke. Even Whitney looked impressed.

"Well, I suppose I could phone him," Mildred said.

Violet smiled. "That would be lovely."

Mildred stood. "Let me see if I can find his card."

She disappeared down a long hall and Whitney leaned toward Violet.

"You're rather determined when you want something, aren't you?" she asked with a smile.

Violet seemed surprised by the comment, but Henry didn't think it was his imagination that she sat a little taller on the sofa. "I suppose so. Although I hope I wasn't rude."

"Not at all," Whitney said. "How are we going to get the things we want if we don't ask for them?"

Violet smiled. "Do you think the man who bought the notebook will sell it to me?"

"I have no idea," Whitney said. "But you'll never know if you don't try. Whatever happens, at least you'll know you did your best."

"You're right," Violet said. "That's something."

Mildred came down the hall holding a business card. "I'm afraid his secretary said he was unavailable." She hesitated, then looked at Whitney. "Do you suppose it's all right to give them the address of his office?"

Whitney looked from Violet to Henry, then back to her grandmother. "They look pretty harmless to me. Besides, it's a business. He can always say no."

"I do love the old things that come my way," Mildred said. "I remember them all like old friends." She had a faraway look, like she was remembering a host of books and knickknacks and postcards and sheet music and art that only she could see. "One has to make a living in this world, but I must confess that I'd rather one of my treasures go to someone who will love it than someone who simply wants to profit off it."

Violet stood. "I can promise you that if I'm able to purchase the notebook, it will be a treasured addition to my family."

Mildred extended her hand with the business card. "His office is in the Empire State Building. I do hope you can reason with him."

Violet's smile was brilliant as she took the business card. She leaned in to give Mildred a hug. "I can't thank you enough!"

"Well, that might be the most enthusiastic form of payment I've had in some time," Mildred said.

Whitney and Violet laughed, but Henry's head was still spinning from everything that had happened. They'd gone from finding the notebook to losing it to possibly finding it again in the past half hour alone. Even more unsettling, as the notebook started to feel closer, he couldn't help feeling that Violet was getting further and further away—and the notebook might be the only way to bring her back.

Twenty-Three

Violet said goodbye to Mildred Appleby with another hug and followed Whitney and Henry out of the apartment and down the stairs. Adrenaline was surging through her body, as if she'd fought a fierce battle instead of attaining a business card that may or may not lead to her father's notebook.

She'd never been so outspoken, had never so firmly stood her ground for something she wanted. The words had seemed to come from someplace deep inside her, a place she hadn't known existed. She'd only known she needed to get the notebook for her father and she would do anything to make it happen.

She was still marveling that it had worked when they stepped onto the sidewalk in front of the building.

"Well, that was even more exciting than I'd anticipated!" Whitney said.

Violet laughed. "For you and me both."

"Would you like me to come with you?" Whitney asked. "I could show you the way."

"It's okay," Violet said, her gaze straying to the silver spire of the Empire State Building. "I think we can find it. Besides, we dragged you right out of work. You must want to get off your feet."

Whitney looked down at her sleek nude heels. "Well, I wouldn't mind getting out of these things, that's for sure."

"You've been so amazing. I'll never be able to thank you enough," Violet said.

"I've loved meeting you!" Whitney said. "We should exchange numbers. That way if you're ever in the city again we can meet up."

"I'd love that." Violet pulled out her phone and

handed it to Whitney, trying to ignore the fact that Henry seemed to be sulking.

She put her number in Whitney's phone and handed it back, then took her own phone and slipped it in her bag.

"Good luck," Whitney said, reaching over to hug her. "Send me a text later and let me know what happened."

"I will," Violet said.

Henry was already edging away, obviously in a hurry to get on with it. Violet couldn't blame him. Their errand had turned out to be more complicated than they'd expected. They should've been on their way to Chelsea Piers by now. Instead, they were still trying to track down the notebook—and getting in more trouble every minute they were dodging Emma and Killian.

She gave Whitney one last wave and joined Henry as he headed down the street toward the Empire State Building. There was a strange and heavy tension between them. It hung like mist, not quite visible but there just the same.

She didn't even try to pretend that things hadn't

shifted between them. She couldn't explain it, but in some ways, it felt like the change had been coming for a long time. She didn't know what it meant, but she had the feeling she was going to have to figure it out sooner rather than later.

"I can't believe she gave me the business card," Violet said, trying to make conversation. They weren't going to figure out the future of their relationship while they were rushing to retrieve her father's notebook.

"Do you think we should take the subway?" Henry asked.

He'd ignored her statement, but she decided to let it go. "The Empire State Building is right there," Violet said, looking up at the shining building. "It might be faster to walk."

"I'm fine with walking." They'd stopped at an intersection and were waiting for the light to change when he turned to look down at her. His expression softened. "That was really awesome back there."

"Do you think so?" she asked, surprised.

He nodded and reached out a hand to touch her

cheek. "I know so. It took a lot of guts to push for the number of the guy who bought the notebook from Mildred."

"Thanks. I kind of surprised myself, too."

"I didn't say I was surprised," Henry said. "You've always been strong, Violet. I'm sorry if I haven't said that enough."

She stood on her tiptoes and kissed him. "It's not your job to make me feel strong, Henry."

She felt the truth of it in her bones. If she hadn't felt strong before, she had no one to blame but herself.

He took her hand as the light changed. They jogged across the intersection, the sounds of the city like a symphony behind them, hope lifting like a brightly colored balloon in her chest. They were close to her father's notebook and for once in her life she felt in control of her own destiny.

She didn't know what it held, but she was beginning to think she was brave enough to find out.

Twenty-Four

Henry should have felt hopeful. Everything was okay between him and Violet, and thanks to her assertiveness at Mildred's they might yet find the notebook before they were forced to head to the hotel.

But he couldn't shake the feeling that their fairy tale in the city was on a collision course with an unhappy ending. It wasn't anything specific Violet had said. She'd even kissed him when he'd told her she was strong.

It was the feeling that the Violet he'd been loving all this time in Storybrooke was actually only a small part of the real Violet. The whole Violet. Like being in the city had somehow unearthed pieces of her that had been there all along but he hadn't known existed.

Maybe they were pieces she hadn't known existed, either.

He and Violet fit together perfectly in Storybrooke. Would they still fit if their pieces changed?

He didn't know.

Not everything is meant to last forever. . . .

He heard his mother's voice on the bus that morning. Had it only been that morning? It seemed like a lifetime ago.

Like a fairy tale ago.

It hurt to think of him and Violet apart. He loved her, and he knew she loved him. They'd shared so many moments, made so many memories. He tried to imagine what his life without Violet would look like and couldn't. She'd occupied a star role in every picture of his future he'd ever imagined since he'd known her.

And yet, he could see her in a place like New York City. He could imagine her going to college and making new friends and figuring out the subway and reinventing herself in a place where she could be more than Sir Morgan's daughter and Henry's girlfriend.

He'd been fooling himself. Storybrooke was never going to be big enough for someone as vibrant and smart and beautiful as Violet. He didn't want to be the person to make her stay.

He wasn't even sure *he* wanted to stay.

The thought took him by surprise. He tried on the idea of starting over someplace new as he and Violet dodged traffic in another busy intersection on their way to the Empire State Building. Could he live somewhere besides Storybrooke? What would it be like not to see his moms every day or go to Granny's Diner or hear Killian's bad jokes or eat his grandmother's cookies warm from the oven?

The idea scared him, but under the fear was something else he thought might be excitement. Where would he go? What would he do there? He'd been telling the truth when he'd told his mom college didn't feel right.

For the first time, he felt like something else—or some-place else—might be calling him.

Of course, heading in different directions didn't mean he and Violet were doomed. Lots of people had long-distance relationships in college. If they could just get the notebook for Violet's father, everything might turn around between them. Then they could talk about mak-ing their future together work no matter what it held.

"Maybe I was wrong," Violet said as they came to a stop at another traffic light. "Maybe we should have taken the subway."

Henry knew what she meant; he felt like they'd already walked a marathon. Trying to pace themselves didn't work. There was something about the city and the briskness of its inhabitants that made it impossible to move slowly. They'd been walking at a slow jog most of the day.

"It's okay," Henry said, his eyes drawn to the loom-ing structure of the Empire State Building. "We're almost there."

He tried not to think about the fact that the rest of

the group was already at Chelsea Piers; he and Violet had missed the entire day and would be lucky to make it back in time for the dinner cruise.

The light changed and they crossed the street, the iconic New York City building appearing bigger and taller as they approached. Finally, they were right there at its doors.

They stopped, both craning their necks to follow the silver column into the sky.

"Wow," Violet said. "It's amazing."

"Yeah, and there's an observation deck at the top." It was yet another thing he would have loved to share with Violet. "I bet you can see the whole city from there."

Violet looked at him with a smile, but before she could respond, another voice rang out across the sidewalk.

"Henry! Violet! Wait!"

They turned toward the familiar voice in time to see a group of people emerging from a yellow taxi at the curb.

It was Killian, Henry's grandmother, and his mom.

And none of them looked happy.

Twenty-Five

Violet's stomach was in knots as they chose a table at Starbucks that would accommodate them all. She was worried about waiting too long to approach the buyer of her father's notebook, but Emma and Mary Margaret had insisted they go somewhere to sit down and talk properly. Violet could hardly object after what she and Henry had put them through.

They found a table and got settled. Emma took a drink of her herbal tea, then drew in a deep breath as she looked at Henry.

"You've got a lot of explaining to do, kid."

Henry nodded. "I know."

Violet couldn't stand the misery on his face. "This isn't Henry's fault," she said. "It's mine."

"Why don't you explain," Mary Margaret said.

Violet bit her lip, trying to find the right words. She'd tried rehearsing the story in her head while they'd waited in line for their drinks, but she'd been too filled with regret over the look of naked relief on Emma's face when she'd pulled Henry into her arms.

Emma had played it cool when she'd texted Henry, but she'd obviously been really worried. The realization made Violet think of her father. The thought of him worrying was like a knife to her heart.

"I will," Violet said. "I promise. But first . . . Have you spoken to my father? I should call and tell him we're okay."

"We didn't call your father," Mary Margaret said. "Yet."

Emma looked at Violet over her tea. "We didn't want to worry him unless it was absolutely necessary. Henry's texts told us you were alive at least. You will have to tell him once we get home."

Violet nodded. "I know. I will."

"You better talk to us first. We've been chasing you around the city all day," Killian said.

"How did you finally find us?" Henry asked, then hurriedly added. "Not that I'm sorry you did. I'm glad."

Emma looked skeptical about the last part. "I've got location tracking on your phone, kid."

"Since when?" Henry asked.

Violet cringed at his indignant tone. They were hardly in a position to be offended by an invasion of privacy.

"Since forever," Emma said. "It's SOP for parents."

"SOP?" Henry asked.

"Standard operating procedure," Killian offered.

"I have it on your line in case of an emergency," Emma said. "I've just never had to use it to track you in Storybrooke."

Killian leaned over the table. "Long story short, we've been three steps behind you all day. Thought for sure we'd catch you sooner, but ran into a couple subway delays, plus one unfortunate run-in with a woman and her nearly feral cat."

"I'm sorry," Violet said. "I had an . . . errand to run. I should never have asked Henry for help."

Emma wasn't sold. "You're going to have to do better than that," she said.

She was right. Violet and Henry owed them more of an explanation.

"You know that before my father was transported to Camelot, he was an engineer?" Violet asked.

"Of course," Mary Margaret said. "He's brilliant at fixing things."

"But he didn't use to simply fix things—he used to invent things. All kinds of things. He had a notebook full of ideas, but it was left behind when he went to Camelot," Violet explained.

"That's intriguing, but what does it have to do with today's ill-advised adventure?" Killian asked.

Violet looked down at the table and traced patterns in the condensation from her iced tea. "My father's been . . . sad lately. He doesn't seem interested in anything and he doesn't work like he used to." She looked up. "But I found it. I found it right here in New York City."

"What did you find?" Emma asked.

"The notebook. The one he left behind when he went to Camelot."

Surprise passed over Mary Margaret's features. "It would have to be over a hundred years old!"

"It is," Violet said. "I found it online at an antiques store."

"How do you know it's his?" Emma asked.

"It's his." Violet leaned forward, her excitement returning. "It has his name and the year 1887—two years before he came to Camelot. I recognize the handwriting. It's filled with his old drawings, his notes, everything!"

"So, you were going to buy the notebook?" Mary Margaret asked. "Is that something you can even afford?"

"I don't know," Violet admitted. "That's something I should have checked before we left Storybrooke. But you see, this isn't Henry's fault. I was worried about getting around the city alone, so I asked Henry to help me."

"That's not true," Henry said. "She's just trying to cover for me. I offered to help. She didn't want me to do it because she knew I'd get in trouble, but I wouldn't take no for an answer. If you want to blame someone, blame me."

"Was it a bloody scavenger hunt?" Killian asked. "You've covered so much ground you could have walked back to Storybrooke by now."

"Yeah, what was with Central Park?" Emma asked. "And Tiffany on Fifth Avenue?"

"It's a long story," Henry said.

"Did you get it?" Mary Margaret asked. "The notebook?"

Violet's shoulders sagged. "No. The woman who advertised it online sold it three days ago." She remembered their reason for coming to the Empire State Building. "She gave us the name of the buyer, though. He has an office in—"

"Let me guess," Killian interrupted. "The Empire State Building."

Violet nodded.

"That's why we're here," Henry said. "It's Violet's last chance to try to buy the notebook for her father."

Violet looked at him. She never stopped being surprised by his loyalty. Even with the mess they were in, he was still trying to help her. He was the best friend she'd ever had.

Emma sighed. "I don't love the way you went about this—and you are so grounded—but I understand. We can talk about your punishment when we get home." She stood. "In the meantime, we need to get to the hotel."

Henry stood. "But . . . we can't leave! We haven't gotten the notebook yet. It's just a few feet away!"

"No, it's not," Emma said. "It's in the Empire State Building, which means getting on an elevator and finding the office, not to mention negotiating with this antiques dealer."

"Exactly," Henry said.

Emma crossed her arms. "In case you haven't noticed, the sun is setting. That means everyone else—including the group you ditched today on Ellis Island—is heading to the hotel to get ready for the dinner cruise."

"Can we skip it?" Violet asked. "Or catch up later?"

After all they'd been through to get the notebook, the thought of giving up now was unbearable.

"I know how important this is to you both," Mary Margaret said, "but trust me when I say we've already pulled every available string to keep Mr. Blankenship and Miss Pond from calling Principal Hoffman. Missing the dinner cruise will be pushing our luck, not to mention the fact that the field trip has been down three chaperones for most of the day. It's not fair to everyone else. Plus, there's the issue of your father, Violet."

"My father?" Violet's heart beat faster. "I thought you said you didn't tell him."

"We didn't, but if Mr. Blankenship or Miss Pond get fed up enough to call Principal Hoffman, all bets are off, and I think we can agree it would be better for your father to hear about this little adventure from you."

The thought made Violet sick. First her father would

be worried; getting a call from the school when your daughter was on an overnight field trip could only be bad news. But once he found out she'd disobeyed the rules, he would be furious.

"Of course," Violet said. "It's just that we've come so far. . . ."

Emma sighed. "I'll tell you what . . . let's get back to the hotel and smooth things over with Mr. Blankenship and Miss Pond and the other chaperones. We'll go on the dinner cruise as planned and I'll see if I can work a little magic for tomorrow."

"You'd bring us back before the bus leaves tomorrow?" Henry asked.

"I can't promise anything, kid, but I'll try," Emma said.

It wasn't what Violet had hoped for, but it was better than nothing.

"Come on." Killian draped one arm around her shoulders and the other around Henry's. "Everything always looks better at sea."

Twenty-Six

Henry waved goodbye to Violet as she got off the elevator with his grandmother at the hotel. Mary Margaret was going to show Violet her room while Emma and Killian took Henry to his on the assigned boys' floor. He wondered if Violet would get a private lecture from his grandma. Henry was counting on one from his mom.

They rose to the next floor in silence. When they stepped off the elevator, Killian turned to Emma. "I'll see you in the room."

She nodded and he headed down the hall with a spring in his step.

Henry envied Killian his carefree nature. He'd spent all day chasing them around the city with Emma and Mary Margaret and he seemed like he didn't have a worry in the world.

Then again, what did Killian have to worry about? Henry was the one in trouble.

"Come on." Emma looked at one of the key cards that had been left for them at the front desk when Mr. Blankenship checked in the rest of the students. "Your room's this way."

They walked halfway down the hall and stopped at a room marked with the number 2134. Henry held out his hand for the card.

"Not so fast," she said, looking into his eyes. "You really scared me today, Henry."

He sighed. "I know. I'm sorry, Mom."

"I just want you to know you can talk to me," she said.

"I do," he said. "It's just that it wasn't my secret, you know? It was Violet's."

Emma touched his shoulder. "I understand, but you can't ever disappear like that again. Deal?"

He nodded. "Deal."

She hugged him a little tighter than usual and handed him the key card. "The bus is leaving for the harbor in forty minutes. You'll have to hurry."

"I will."

He slid the card into the door, waited for the light to turn green, and stepped into the hotel room. Drew was lying on the bed in slacks and no shirt while he looked at his phone. He sat up quickly.

"I thought maybe you'd made a run for it," he said.

"Where would I go?" Henry asked, dropping his backpack next to his duffel. "Thanks for grabbing my duffel."

"Sure. Where were you?" Drew asked, running a hand through his messy hair.

"Just around the city," Henry said. "I was helping Violet with something."

"I hope it was worth it," Drew said. "I thought Mr.

Blankenship was going to lose it when he found out you were gone."

Henry thought about that. Had it been worth it? They hadn't gotten the notebook, but he'd proven to Violet that she could count on him no matter what, and they'd had a little fun along the way in spite of the weirdness between them.

"It was worth it," he said.

"What was worth it?" Paul said, emerging from the bathroom with wet hair.

"Pissing off Mr. Blankenship," Drew said.

"I'd do that for nothing," Paul said, crossing the room to his suitcase.

Henry and Drew laughed.

It was nice to be back with his friends. He'd enjoyed his time alone with Violet, but if he was being honest with himself, it had also been kind of overwhelming to be responsible for getting them around the city and finding her father's notebook. The weight of responsibility had been heavier than he'd expected. It was almost a relief to be back within the confines of normal rules where the adults took care of everything. It wouldn't last—in a year he'd be on his own one way or another—but it was nice to sink back into the safety of adolescence for a while longer.

"You better hurry," Drew said. "Bus is leaving soon."

"Unless you're going like that," Paul added.

Henry looked down at his dirty jeans and limp T-shirt. "No, I'm definitely not."

He went to his duffel and removed the slacks and dress shirt he'd packed for the dinner cruise. "You guys done with the bathroom?"

"It's all yours," Drew said, already back on his phone.

Henry took his stuff into the bathroom and shut the door. He washed up quickly, then replaced his street clothes with the dress clothes. He spent a few minutes fixing his hair in the mirror, pausing to look at his reflection. What did Violet see when she looked at him?

A kid? A man?

What did he see when he looked at himself?

He didn't know. He felt like a little of both. It used to be enough for Violet, but he had the feeling that might not be true anymore.

He stood straighter and finished buttoning his shirt. The chaos of the day had turned everything upside down, including his relationship with Violet. Tonight would be different. There would be no rushing for the subway or arguing over directions. They would get on the bus with everyone else, get off the bus at the harbor, and board the boat. The chaperones would make all the decisions and he and Violet would eat and laugh and dance under the stars against the backdrop of the city she loved.

He would hold her close and she would look at him like she used to. Like he was everything she needed. Like she wasn't already planning her escape—not only from Storybrooke, but from him.

Twenty-Seven

Violet was relieved when Mary Margaret dropped her at the hotel room without another word about the day's misadventure. She was still reeling from the possible loss of her father's notebook—especially when she'd been so close to getting it—and from everything that had happened with Henry.

Sadie and Lizette squealed as she entered the room. They launched a hurricane of questions at her as she set down her bag. Sadie led her to the bed and forced her to sit.

"Tell us everything," she said, eyes shining.

"Yeah, like, every single thing," Lizette added.

Violet laughed. "I have to get ready."

"Give us the short version," Lizette begged. "Seriously, today was so boring—except for the bowling alley, when Ashley Milton lost control of her ball and almost decapitated an old guy in the lane next to her."

"Are you serious?" Violet asked.

"She is," Sadie said. "It would have been funny if it hadn't been such a close call. But that's not what we want to talk about. Tell us all about your day with Henry!"

"It wasn't like that," Violet said, even though in the beginning, a big part of her excitement had been about spending time with Henry. "I was trying to find something for my father."

"What is it?" Lizette asked.

Violet thought about it, not wanting to lie. "A family heirloom. I spotted it online at an antiques shop in the city. I wanted to bring it back for him."

"And did you get it?" Sadie asked.

Violet shook her head. "Not yet."

"Wait . . . You're not making another break for it tomorrow while we're at the Met, are you?" Sadie asked. "Because I have a feeling they're going to be watching you and Henry like hawks."

"I don't know," Violet said. "Henry's mom said she would talk to Mr. Blankenship and see if she could come with us at some point."

"And what about Henry?" Sadie asked. "Was it super exciting and romantic to be in the city alone?"

"It was . . . nice," Violet said.

Lizette looked surprised. "Nice?"

"Yeah, nice." Violet stood. "I have to get ready. We have less than a half hour before we have to be in the lobby, and I'm a mess."

She tried to ignore the meaningful lift of Sadie's eyebrows as she went to her overnight bag to pull out the dress she'd brought for the dinner cruise. She couldn't even explain the situation with Henry to herself. There was no way she could explain it to Sadie and Lizette.

She took her dress and toiletries into the bathroom.

After stripping to her underwear, she washed up as best she could and slipped the dress over her head, then studied herself in the mirror.

The dress's deep raspberry silk set off her dark hair and pale skin, the sweetheart neckline drawing attention to her collarbone and long neck. The bodice was fitted through the waist, then flared slightly around her knees. It was the nicest dress she owned and she'd been over the moon about the prospect of wearing it for the dinner cruise with Henry. Now she couldn't help thinking it was a little provincial.

She thought about all the dresses she'd seen as she and Henry had made their way through the city. There had been simple shifts and elegant couture, flowing vintage dresses from the '70s with deep necklines, and tiny minis that would have hugged every curve of her body.

It wasn't that she coveted them because they were new. It was more about the fact that they were different. They might not be her taste when all was said and done, but she suddenly didn't know if the dress she was actually wearing was her taste, either.

In fact, she wasn't sure of much anymore. That day in the city had only confused who she was and what she wanted—or maybe it had just uncovered the confusion that had already been there.

More and more she was beginning to understand her uncertainty wasn't about Henry at all; it was about her.

It was about who she was underneath the expectations of everyone who thought they knew her. How was she supposed to figure that out within the confines of those expectations? How much of her personality was really her? How much of it was a result of living up to what was expected of her?

Did she let Henry take charge because he expected her to let him take charge? Did she dress the way she did because she actually liked her clothes or because it was the way everyone thought she should dress, because everyone would question her if she wore something they thought was out of character? Did she keep her hair long because she liked it or because everyone in Storybrooke would be shocked if she cut it?

She tried to imagine going to school in heels, funky

pants, and shrunken T-shirts, her hair short and swingy like Whitney Day's. She would wear eyeliner that curved up at the corners of her eyes and lipstick that brought out the color in her cheeks.

It would be impossible. Everyone would stare and whisper. They'd wonder if she'd lost her mind, and that was if she could get out of the house without her dad raising a fuss.

"You okay, Vee?" Sadie asked from the other side of the bathroom door. "We have to get to the lobby."

"I'm good," Violet said. "I'm coming."

She gathered up her stuff and opened the door, then hurried to her bag for her dress shoes. Tonight she was Henry's girlfriend, her dad's reliable daughter, and Storybrooke High's straight-A student.

She didn't know who she would be tomorrow or next year, but maybe admitting she didn't know was the first step in finding out.

Twenty-Eight

Henry stepped off the bus and joined Violet by the railing that overlooked the Hudson. She looked as beautiful as he'd ever seen her—and that was saying a lot, because Violet was the most beautiful girl he'd ever seen every day of the week.

She looked out over the water and took a deep breath of the salty air. "This is amazing!"

The skyscrapers were lit up and rising into the sky, their lights casting jeweled reflections onto the water. "It really is."

She opened her mouth to say something, then closed it.

"What?" Henry asked.

She shook her head. "Nothing."

"It's okay," he said softly. "It's beautiful. I'm glad you're enjoying it."

"You are?"

He nodded, feeling like a jerk for the way he'd acted earlier. "Of course. I always want you to be happy, Violet. I . . . well, I hope you know that."

She smiled. "I do."

Jack, Matthew, Ruth, and Melody joined them by the railing as the bus continued to empty. Henry didn't think he was imagining the tension in the air. Clearly, he and Violet weren't done apologizing for the day.

"Hey," he said, looking at them, "I'm really sorry we bailed on you guys at Ellis. I hope it didn't ruin your day."

Jack shrugged. "It's cool."

"They had to reassign us," Matthew said accusingly.

"I'm sorry," Henry said. "It wasn't okay for us to leave like we did. What we had to do was important, but that's no excuse."

"Don't be mad at Henry," Violet said. "It was really

my fault. He was helping me with something. I'm sorry if it ruined your day."

"It's okay," Ruth said. "We still got to see everything."

"Did you get in trouble?" Melody asked.

Henry laughed. "Does being grounded for life count?"

Emma hadn't said it, but he knew it was pretty much a foregone conclusion.

"Whatever you did, it had to be better than all those creepy statues at the wax museum," Jack said.

Everyone laughed.

Mary Margaret stood in front of the group with her clipboard in hand. She'd changed into a dress and looked as calm as ever in spite of the fact that she'd started the day before the sun came up and had spent the rest of it chasing him and Violet around the city with Emma and Killian. She and Emma had been separated when Emma was a baby, but Emma definitely got her cool head from Mary Margaret. There were no two people he'd rather have by his side in any crisis.

"Okay, everyone," she said. "Stay with your groups

until you get on the boat. We'll do another count then."

Emma stepped next to him and Henry smiled at her. "You look nice, Mom."

"Yeah?" She looked down at the simple black dress she was wearing.

"Yeah."

"Thanks, kid." She moved to ruffle his hair, then seemed to think better of it.

"'Nice'?" Killian said, draping an arm around her. "I have the most beautiful date in the group."

Killian looked pretty fancy himself, even if he was wearing boots with his suit.

"Flattery will get you everywhere," Emma said, kissing Killian's cheek.

"Everywhere but that boat," he said. "Let's go."

Emma took his hand and they got into the line waiting to board the boat. Henry leaned over the railing, wanting to get a glimpse of it. He wasn't disappointed.

The enormous yacht tied up at the dock had three levels and at least as many decks. Through the windows, he could see the staff moving around, making preparations for the dinner cruise. Inside, the lights changed from soft yellow to blue to purple and back again. Music spilled out of the open windows, already setting the scene for the night ahead.

The line started moving and a cool breeze blew off the water. Henry felt a lifting of his earlier worry as they headed for the ramp that would take them onto the boat. He took Violet's hand and she looked up at him with a smile.

He didn't know what would happen when they got back to Storybrooke. He didn't even know what would happen tomorrow.

But tonight, he had Violet's hand in his. Tonight, they would pretend that everything could stay the same forever.

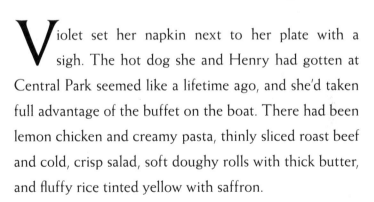

Twenty-Nine

Violet set her napkin next to her plate with a sigh. The hot dog she and Henry had gotten at Central Park seemed like a lifetime ago, and she'd taken full advantage of the buffet on the boat. There had been lemon chicken and creamy pasta, thinly sliced roast beef and cold, crisp salad, soft doughy rolls with thick butter, and fluffy rice tinted yellow with saffron.

And then there were the desserts: chocolate mousse and delicate cake and puffy éclairs filled with Bavarian cream.

"I can't eat another bite," Henry said, next to her.

"I can't even look at another bite," Violet said.

They'd spent the first half hour nibbling appetizers on the top deck as the boat moved away from the harbor. The farther they'd gotten from land, the freer Violet had felt. Being on the boat was like floating on a cloud, the cool evening breeze like wind under wings she could almost believe she had.

Once they were out on the river they'd moved belowdecks for dinner. Spirits were high, and except for a stern glance from Mr. Blankenship, no one seemed to hold Henry and Violet's earlier escape against them.

They'd eaten with Sadie, Lizette, Drew, Paul, Ruth, Melody, and Jack, laughing and talking about their day. Everyone on the field trip shared the highlights of Ellis Island, the wax museum, and bowling—including a detailed account of Ashley's rogue bowling ball—and Henry and Violet told them about the ballet dancers in the street, the hot dogs at Central Park, the glamour of Tiffany on Fifth Avenue.

Violet looked up as the music streaming from the speakers changed from soft background music to something familiar with a noticeable bass line and an insistent beat.

"You know what this means, right?" Henry asked, looking at her.

"Oh, no," she said. "It's not . . ."

He nodded and stood, then held out his hand. "It's time to dance."

She laughed. "I'm stuffed!"

"Me too," he said. "Moving is good for digestion. That's what Regina always says, anyway."

She took his hand. "I suppose I'll take Regina's word for it."

They left the dining area and made their way up onto the first deck. The music got louder as they moved under the white lights strung overhead. Then they were enveloped in the crowd, Sadie, Lizette, and Drew pulling them into their circle. Violet moved with the music, watching as Drew and Henry made up silly dance moves until they were all doubled over with laughter.

It was like being in a dream, drifting through the darkness on their island of laughter and music, the city lights rising beyond the water like a series of Technicolor castles.

She was out of breath by the time the music finally

slowed down. The dance floor quickly cleared, leaving only a handful of couples and some of the chaperones, including Emma and Killian.

Henry held out his hand. Violet took it and he pulled her into his arms as he started swaying to the music.

It wasn't the first time they'd slow-danced together, but Violet immediately sensed that it was somehow different. It wasn't Henry; he was as real and solid as he'd ever been. It wasn't even the boat or the city in the distance, although those things were definitely new.

It took her a few minutes to realize that the only thing different was her.

She wasn't the same Violet who'd come to Storybrooke from Camelot. She wasn't even the same Violet who'd been living in Storybrooke the past year. She'd changed somewhere along the line.

Being with Henry had been easy since the very beginning. They'd fallen into habits and patterns without thinking, had been fooled into believing it could stay that way forever.

But she knew better than anyone that nothing stayed the same forever. Some changes you saw coming, and others took you by surprise, but change was inevitable.

She understood her father's sadness better now. He'd twice had to say goodbye, to people and belongings and even ways of doing things. He'd done it with his head held high, but if the pain in Violet's heart at the thought of saying goodbye to Henry was any indication, it had been a lot harder than her father had let on.

Did she have the same courage? Could she say goodbye to the people and places she loved even when it hurt? Because it *would* hurt. She knew it beyond a shadow of a doubt as she breathed in the scent of the cologne she'd bought Henry for Christmas, as she felt the familiar strength of his shoulder under her hand.

She leaned her head against him and felt his arms tighten around her waist. Closing her eyes, she tried to imprint on her memory the moment when she was floating over the water in Henry's arms. The moment when they still belonged to each other.

Thirty

Henry was standing on the upper deck of the boat, watching the city lights and trying to pick out some of the smaller buildings, when his mom came up next to him.

"Hey," she said.

"Hey."

"I've had about all I can take of Killian's pirate jokes," she said.

He laughed. "You love it and you know it."

"Well, I love *him*," she said. "The bad jokes are just part of the package at this point."

"Small price to pay for love," Henry said.

She looked harder at him. "What's up, Henry?"

"What do you mean?" he asked.

"Come on, kid. I like to think I know you," she said. "Don't rain on my parade."

Henry hesitated. He wanted to tell his mom everything: how Violet seemed sometimes sad and distant, how he felt stupid and incompetent trying to be strong for her without being overbearing, the way it felt like he couldn't do anything right ever since they'd come to the city. He wanted to ask her how he was supposed to be both strong and sensitive, how he was supposed to be Violet's hero and still leave room for her to save herself, too.

"Things didn't exactly go as planned today," he said.

"Tell me about it."

"I mean, when it comes to getting the notebook," Henry said.

"I know," she said, "but it doesn't sound like any of that was your fault."

They'd filled her in on the finer details of the day during the cab ride from the coffee shop to the hotel.

He drew in a breath. "It's not just the notebook and all the trouble we've had tracking it down. It's . . . well, it's Violet."

Understanding lit Emma's eyes, and he suddenly wondered if she'd seen it all coming, if the signs that had been invisible to him in Storybrooke had been obvious to someone like Emma, who had a lot more life experience than Henry.

"I see," she said. "Want to talk about it?"

He shrugged. "I don't know what to say. She just seems . . . far away. She really likes it here, and I don't think I do."

"You don't have to agree on everything to love someone," Emma said. "But I have a feeling there's more to it than Violet's feelings about the city."

"I think maybe she wants to be alone for a while." He'd been thinking it ever since they'd left Tiffany, but saying it out loud made it real.

"What about you?" she asked. "What do you want?"

"I want Violet," he said without hesitation. "But not like this. Not if it's not good for her or if it doesn't make her happy."

She squeezed his shoulder. "That's a pretty awesome thing to say, Henry."

"It doesn't feel awesome," he said.

"I know, but that's part of why it's so great that you said it." She looked into his eyes. "That's what love is, Henry. It's doing things for someone because you love them, even when it's hard. That includes letting go."

"But if I love her, why does it have to end?" He felt naive asking the question, like a kid asking why Santa Claus wasn't real. "And why did she have to stop loving me?"

"Oh, Henry . . . Violet hasn't stopped loving you. Anyone can see that. But the thing is, loving someone doesn't mean things will always be the same. You can love someone and still need time apart. You can even love someone and discover that you're not meant to be together."

He remembered her words from the bus. "Not everything's meant to last forever?"

"Exactly. But that doesn't mean it isn't real," she said.

He knew she was right, but it still felt like a giant hand was squeezing his heart. He didn't want to say goodbye to Violet, didn't want to imagine their relationship ending.

"That sucks," he said.

She nodded. "It does. Is there anything I can do?"

He didn't even have to think about it. "Can you let me go alone with Violet to get the notebook tomorrow?" he asked. "I'd just really like to be her hero on this one."

"You could be *my* hero by not scaring me half to death again," she said.

"Deal," he said. "But seriously, can you let me do it on my own?"

"I'm not even sure I can get you both away from the group. I've been waiting for Mr. Blankenship to have another glass of wine to ask about it." She sighed. "But if we can manage it, I think Killian and I could wait at the coffee shop while you and Violet see about the notebook."

"Really?"

"Really."

"Thanks, Mom," he said.

"Is this where we hug?" she asked. "Will it cramp your style? Because I'd really like to hug my awesome kid right now."

He laughed and submitted to a hug that wasn't half bad.

"Hey, Mom?" he asked when they pulled apart.

"Yeah?"

"Can I ask you for one more favor?"

She laughed a little. "Was that hug to soften me up?"

"Not at all," he said. "I liked it. I promise."

"You can always ask," she said.

He leaned in and tried to explain.

Thirty-One

Violet watched as the man behind the counter lifted a steaming hot waffle from the iron and set it on her plate. Her mouth watered as the smell of crispy dough and hot oil hit her nose.

"Thank you," she said.

He nodded. "Welcome."

She continued down the waffle bar and added heaps of butter, syrup, and fresh strawberries, plus a dab of whipped cream for good measure. When she was done she carried her plate to the table she was sharing with Sadie and Lizette. She was putting the first delicious bite into her mouth when they returned with their plates.

"Did you see the omelet station?" Sadie said, sliding into the seat across from Violet.

Violet shook her head while she chewed. She'd been too excited about the waffle bar to look at much else.

"They can make you an omelet with anything," Sadie said. "Like, literally anything."

Violet glanced at the omelet on Sadie's plate. Cheese oozed out of the sides along with little pieces of what looked like pepper and tomato.

"It looks amazing," Violet said.

"What looks amazing?" Lizette said, taking the seat next to Sadie.

"My omelet," Sadie said.

Lizette started spreading cream cheese on her bagel. "Yuck. I hate eggs."

"Your loss," Sadie said, shoving a bite into her mouth.

Violet couldn't help feeling nostalgic. How many conversations had she, Sadie, and Lizette had just like this one? How many times had they talked about parents and school and boys? Would they stay friends after they went

their separate ways after high school? Or would everything change like it was changing for her and Henry?

"Why so quiet, Vee?" Sadie asked.

"I was just thinking about how much I love you guys,
and how much I'm going to miss you after high school,"
she said.

"That's crazy talk," Lizette said with a wave of her
fork. "We'll always be friends."

"Promise?" Violet said.

"Are you serious?" Sadie asked. "How could you
doubt it?"

Violet sighed. "I don't know. It's being in the city. It's
made me weird about everything."

Sadie put down her fork and tucked a piece of hair
behind one ear. "Weird how?"

Violet drew in a breath. "Just . . . confused, I guess.
Or maybe *not* confused for the first time in a long time."

"Now I'm confused," Lizette said.

Sadie shot her a glance. "You're always confused."

Lizette nodded, her ponytail bobbing. "True."

Sadie turned her attention back to Violet. "Seriously, what are you talking about?"

Violet considered all that had happened, all the things she'd realized over the past two days. There wasn't time to rehash it all. She'd have to give them the short version instead.

"Being here has made me realize I'm ready to leave Storybrooke," she said. "Not now, obviously, but after high school."

"Duh," Lizette said. "I've been ready to leave Storybrooke since third grade."

Violet laughed. "Well, I didn't know. I thought maybe . . ."

"Maybe?" Sadie prompted.

"I guess I thought maybe I would be there forever, or maybe I'd go to a nearby college for four years and then come back," Violet said.

"What about now?" Lizette asked.

"Now I think I need to put some serious distance between myself and Storybrooke."

"What about Henry?" Lizette asked.

Violet bit her lip, her gaze straying to the other side of the room, where Henry was having breakfast with Drew and Paul. "I don't know. I haven't figured that out."

It wasn't entirely true, but Violet still didn't know how she was going to talk to Henry about the way she felt. She definitely couldn't explain it to Sadie and Lizette. Not yet, anyway.

"Long-distance relationships never last," Lizette said, popping a bite of her bagel into her mouth. "Remember when Ben Linton moved to Boston and we promised we'd get married after high school?"

"Everyone remembers you and Ben Linton," Sadie said. "You won't let us forget it."

"Right," Lizette said. "And do you remember that he texted me exactly eight times and called once before he dropped off the face of the earth?"

"Just because Ben Linton ghosted you doesn't mean Henry would do that to Violet," Sadie said.

"I'm just saying," Lizette said.

Sadie looked sharply at her. "Well, don't."

"What about you guys?" Violet was eager to change

the subject. "What do you think you'll do after senior year?"

Lizette shrugged. "I haven't thought about it much. We still have a whole year."

"That's true," Violet said.

"I think I'm going to apply to MIT," Sadie said. "I'm pretty sure I can get in if I get my Draft and Design grade up."

"I'm sure you can," Violet said. Sadie had always loved building things. When she and Lizette had opted for Studio Art to fulfill their design elective, Sadie had chosen Draft and Design and shown a natural talent for architecture.

"I don't know what I'd do with the degree," Sadie said, "but I can figure out that part later."

"I'm just going to figure it all out later," Lizette said, standing with her coffee cup in hand. "Anyone want a refill?"

Sadie and Violet declined and Lizette headed toward the coffee bar. Lizette might not have everything figured out yet, but Violet knew she'd be just fine. In fact, she had the sudden feeling they would all be fine. They were taking different paths through the woods, but somehow they would all make it through to the other side.

"Violet, can I speak to you for a sec?"

Violet looked up to find Emma looking down at her.

"Sure." Violet moved to get up and Sadie slid out of the booth.

"Take my seat," Sadie said. "I'm finished anyway. I want to brush my teeth before we leave."

Violet wasn't surprised. Sadie had been obsessed with brushing her teeth since she'd gotten her braces off in tenth grade.

"Thanks, Sadie," Emma said.

"Sure." Sadie turned to Violet. "See you on the bus."

"Yeah, see you."

Emma waited until Sadie was out of earshot to speak. "Mr. Blankenship has agreed to let Killian and me take you and Henry while everyone else is at the Met, as long as we're back in time to catch the bus home."

"Really?" Violet could hardly contain her excitement. The notebook wasn't out of reach after all.

"Really," Emma said. "I did have to call your dad to give Mr. Blankenship his permission, but I didn't mention anything about yesterday. I'll let you do that when we get home."

Violet nodded, more than a little surprised her father had given his permission without wanting to speak directly to Violet. Then again, he trusted Emma and Killian more than most people.

"I will, I promise," Violet said. "This means so much to me. I can't thank you enough."

Emma smiled. "Getting that notebook for your dad is all the thanks I need. If you give me the antiques dealer's business card, I'll call and make sure he's in the office before we head over there."

Violet reached into her bag and handed the card to Emma.

"We'll take a taxi," Emma said. "I'll get Henry and meet you in the lobby in ten minutes."

Thirty-Two

Henry could hardly contain his excitement as the taxi weaved through morning traffic. The city was clogged with cars and buses and delivery trucks, and the sound of honking horns pinged off the buildings that were filling with people, ready for a new day.

He glanced over at his mom, who was sitting next to the other window across the back seat while Killian occupied the passenger seat next to the taxi driver. Henry hadn't been sure she would agree to his mission; he hadn't even been sure she would be able to get them away from the field trip to continue their hunt for the notebook. She'd really come through for him, though, and he was beginning to realize he owed her big time. He was under no illusion that their surprise stop would change anything between him and Violet, but it felt important to do it anyway, not because he wanted something from Violet but because he wanted something *for* her.

The taxi took a right turn so hard that Violet reached out to clutch his hand. He squeezed her hand in solidarity and tried to keep his expression calm. He'd already seen his life pass in front of his eyes more than once on the drive from the hotel, but there was no reason Violet had to know that.

No wonder New Yorkers took the subway everywhere.

The car slowed and they came to a stop near a corner. Emma leaned over Violet to look at Henry.

"That way," she said, pointing to a shady street beyond the taxi's windows.

Violet leaned down to look past Henry out the

window. "Where's the Empire State Building? I don't see it."

"I have something to show you real quick," Henry said, opening the door. "Don't worry. It won't take long."

Violet glanced back at Emma. "It's okay?"

Emma smiled. "It's okay. We'll be right here."

Violet slid from the car and Henry closed the door behind her, then took her hand.

"What is this, Henry? We're supposed to be getting the notebook," she said.

"We're going to, I promise," he said. "Just trust me."

They made their way down a shady street, trees towering overhead. It felt like a secret part of the city, the traffic like the background music at a nice restaurant: muffled and soothing. Brick buildings lined both sides of the street, and though they were in good repair, Henry had the feeling they'd been there a long time.

"I don't understand," Violet said as they reached the end of the street. "What is this . . . Oh!"

Her hand flew to her mouth as she took in the

enormous patchwork lawn leading to a massive domed building fronted with pillars. All around them students walked with backpacks and messenger bags. Some of them had headphones in their ears, while others talked and laughed in groups.

"Is this . . . ?"

"Columbia University?" Henry said. "Yes. Yes, it is."

He couldn't keep the smile from springing to his lips. In fact, he wasn't sure he'd smiled so hard since they'd left Storybrooke. It had nothing at all to do with the scene in front of them and everything to do with Violet's reaction.

He grinned. "Come on. We don't have a lot of time."

They walked across the massive quad and up one of the pathways leading to the big domed building.

"This is unbelievable," Violet said. "It's like a little city inside a bigger city."

"It is kind of crazy," he said.

On their way up the wide steps that led to the front of the domed building, they passed a statue of a seated woman wearing a leafy crown, her arms outstretched toward the grassy quad. When they reached the top of the steps, Henry stopped.

"Want to sit?" he asked.

"Do we have time?" Violet asked.

"I think so," Henry said. "My mom called Basil Knaggs's office and his secretary said he would be in all day."

"Okay," she said, taking a seat.

He lowered himself onto the step next to her and they sat in silence for a few moments. Henry watched the students crisscrossing the lawn and tried to picture Violet among them. It wasn't hard at all. He could see her—maybe in different clothes and with different hair, but still kind, smart, strong Violet.

"Why did you bring me here, Henry?" she asked quietly.

He didn't dare look at her. "I wanted you to see one of your dreams up close. I guess . . . well, I guess I just wanted you to see yourself here, and I wanted you to know I can see you here, too."

"You can?" she asked.

He turned to look at her. "Of course I can. It makes me sad that you don't know that."

She took a deep breath and looked at the scene around them. "Don't take it personally. It's all me. I think I got so used to being scared that I forgot I wasn't always that way. It's not your job to help me remember, although it doesn't surprise me that you would." She turned to look at him. "You've been so good to me, Henry."

He tried not to hear the past tense in the statement, tried not to read any finality in it. Maybe if he could make Violet see that he supported her no matter what— even if she went away to school—they could figure out how to make it work between them.

"It's not hard to be good to you, and it's not some kind of favor," he said. "You deserve to have people be good to you, Violet. You deserve everything."

She smiled. "So do you, Henry."

She leaned in to kiss him and he closed his eyes and tried to pretend he hadn't seen the sadness in her smile, hadn't heard the goodbye in her words.

Thirty-Three

The image of Columbia University was imprinted on Violet's mind as they rode to the Empire State Building. She'd been able to see herself there, had been able to see herself among the other students heading to class.

Had been able to see herself without Henry.

She took a deep breath. She would have to think about the future later. Right now, she needed to get the notebook for her father. Once she had it in her hands, she would find a way to talk to Henry, to explain that she wasn't sure she could figure out who she was when every time she looked at him she saw a version of herself in his eyes that she wasn't sure was real.

"Mr. Knaggs's secretary should be expecting you," Emma said.

"Thanks for calling him," Violet said.

In some ways, it was a relief to be back in the presence of adults like Emma and Killian who somehow seemed to have all the answers—even if Killian's answers were usually delivered with a dose of corny humor or snarky comment.

But they were also a reminder of her real life, a life that seemed even smaller from the streets of a city like Manhattan than it seemed from the windows of Storybrooke. She wasn't ready to go back, and she suddenly couldn't wait until after graduation, when she would be able to step into a whole new life—assuming, of course, that she found her father's notebook.

She looked over at Henry and felt a rush of affection. So much had seemed to change between them over the past two days, but he'd still gone to bat for her both with

his mom and by taking her to Columbia that morning.
Now he was giving up his last day of the field trip to help
her find her father's notebook.

That part was important all of a sudden, that she and
Henry find the notebook together. She didn't know what
was in the cards for them after this, but it seemed right
that they would end their journey the way they started
it: together.

The taxi pulled over to the side of the street and
Killian paid the driver while Henry, Violet, and Emma
filed out of the car. A couple minutes later, Killian joined
them on the sidewalk.

"We'll be in the coffee shop," Emma said. "Text or
call if you need anything."

"You're not coming with us?" Violet asked.

After their escape the day before, it seemed too good
to be true that Emma would let them out of her sight not
once, but twice in the same morning.

Emma shook her head. "You and Henry started this,
you should finish it. Besides, I think you can handle it

just fine without us." She looked at Henry. "But seriously, Henry, if you pull anything stupid, the grounding you've already earned will look like a vacation."

He nodded. "I get it. We'll go into the office, see about the notebook, and then we'll be back out, I promise."

She gave him a quick hug. "Good luck, kid." Violet couldn't help feeling there was some kind of hidden meaning to the words. "Good luck, Violet."

"Thank you," Violet said, looking from Emma to Killian. "I'm so grateful."

"No worries," Emma said. "Just get the notebook so we can get back to the field trip before Mr. Blankenship bans me from chaperoning forever."

She and Killian started down the street to the coffee shop and Henry and Violet headed for the door of the Empire State Building. They were almost there when Violet pulled Henry aside.

"Is everything okay?" he asked, his brow furrowed with concern.

"I wanted to say thank you," she said.

"For what?" Henry asked.

"For everything," she said. "For ditching the field trip and getting in trouble and crisscrossing this crazy city in search of something we may never find and taking me to Columbia this morning."

"You don't have to thank me, Violet. I'll always be here if you need me."

Her throat closed with emotion. She couldn't find the words to say all the things she wanted—needed—to say. Anyway, now wasn't the time.

"Still," she said. "Thank you."

"Don't thank me yet," he said. "We still need to get the notebook."

She drew in a breath. This was it. Their last chance.

"Let's go," she said.

They approached the front of the building and stopped to look up at the gleaming facade. It seemed to stretch even beyond the clouds. Three panes of glass adorned with gold Art Deco trim decorated the front of the building over three sets of doors. Stone columns flanked the glass on both sides and an American flag waved proudly in the wind over the words EMPIRE STATE.

"I can't believe we're actually here," Henry said.

"It's even bigger up close," Violet said.

He looked at her. "Let's go get your father's notebook."

She stepped into the revolving door and emerged in the lobby, a gleaming rectangle filled with amber light and tile polished to a high gloss. Velvet rope marked the elevators to the observation decks. Beyond them, at the end of the hall, a monument to the building shone like a beacon.

"Wow," Violet said.

"I'll second that," Henry said. "Where's the business card?"

Violet tore her gaze away from the spectacle and pulled out the business card Mildred Appleby had given her, glad Emma had returned it after calling Basil Knaggs's office that morning.

"'Basil Knaggs Art and Ephemera,'" she read. "Number fifty-two sixty-eight."

"Does that mean the fifty-second floor?" Henry asked.

"That would be my guess," Violet said.

"Let's give it a shot," Henry said, heading for the elevators.

The elevator doors were sleek and black. Violet had the sense she was stepping into history. She could almost see the same doors decades ago, the same grand hallway back when the Empire State Building was first erected.

One set of doors opened almost immediately. Violet and Henry stepped into the elevator car and were followed by a young woman carrying a tray of coffees and an older man in a tweed suit. Henry pressed the button for the fifty-second floor and they began rising smoothly into the air.

Violet couldn't help noticing that no one spoke to them. She knew in some places it might be considered rude, but after being in Storybrooke, where she couldn't stop at the grocery store for bread without engaging in a conversation with someone about her father, school, or the upcoming Strawberry Festival, she found it relaxing.

There was no pressure to be friendly or witty, no worry about offending someone if she wasn't in the mood to talk. She felt as if a weight had been lifted from her shoulders, one she hadn't realized she'd been carrying.

The young woman with the coffee exited first. A few seconds later, the man in tweed stepped out of the elevator and Henry smiled down at Violet as the car continued its ascent. She took his hand, then fought a rush of sadness when she saw his surprise.

Did he think she didn't love him anymore? The thought was unbearable. Couldn't she love Henry and want some space for herself at the same time? Would it be possible to stay friends if they ended their romantic relationship?

She was prevented from trying to find the answers when the elevator doors opened onto the fifty-second floor. They stepped out into a surprisingly nondescript hallway. It might have been any hall in any office building instead of one in the most iconic building in New York City.

Henry walked to the first office and read from a plaque on the wall next to the door. "Fifty-two forty-four." He looked at Violet. "Let's try this way."

They started down the hall, watching as the numbers next to the doors rose.

5256 . . . 5258 . . . 5260 . . .

Finally, they came to 5268. A sign on the glass read BASIL KNAGGS ART AND EPHEMERA, NEW YORK CITY.

"This is the place," Henry said.

Violet touched her stomach as if that would calm the butterflies fluttering there. "I'm so nervous," she confessed.

He smiled. "Don't be. He's obviously a dealer who just wants to make money on the notebook. I'm sure we can work something out. Let's go get it."

He opened the door.

Thirty-Four

Henry stepped into the lobby of a simple, modern office and held the door for Violet. Four chairs sat against one wall, facing a reception desk manned by a gray-haired woman with fiery green eyes. She looked up as they entered the office.

"Hello," she said. "How may I help you?"

They approached the desk.

"We're here to see a Mr. Basil Knaggs," Henry said. "My mom called your office this morning."

The woman smiled. "I take it you're Henry and Violet?"

"That's right," Henry said. His mom must have told the secretary their names when she'd called. "We're interested in buying one of his items: a notebook."

She gave them a sympathetic smile. "I'm afraid Mr. Knaggs had to step into a meeting."

Henry could hardly believe his ears. Really? After all they'd been through to get Sir Morgan's notebook, this one thing couldn't go right for them?

"We were told he'd be in all day," Henry said.

"Oh, he's in," the woman said. "There was simply an urgent matter he had to resolve. It was unexpected."

Henry took a deep breath. Violet needed him to be calm. Giving up now wasn't an option, not while there was still hope of getting the notebook.

"Do you know how long he'll be?" Henry asked.

"No more than an hour. You're welcome to wait if you'd like," she said, gesturing to the chairs against the wall.

Henry thought about it. They could wait in the drab office, trying not to stare at Basil Knaggs's receptionist and thinking about how badly cursed their mission to get the notebook seemed to be—but he had a better idea.

"We'll be back," Henry said, taking Violet's hand.

"What are you doing?" Violet asked when they got out into the hall. "We have to wait!"

He put his hands on her face and gave her a quick kiss. "I promise we'll be back in an hour. Come on!"

He pulled her down the hall toward the elevators and pressed the down button.

"I don't understand," Violet said. "Why are we going back down?"

Henry laughed. "Has anyone ever told you you're not an easy person to surprise?"

She gave him an exaggerated sigh. "Fine. No more questions."

They descended to the lobby and Henry followed the signs to the ticket booth. He was surprised the line wasn't longer, but then he remembered it was the middle of a weekday in May. At least one thing had gone right;

if they'd come on the weekend or in the middle of summer, the line probably would have been a lot longer.

Henry got in line behind a couple with three kids and removed his wallet.

"Henry Mills, are you taking me to the top of the Empire State Building?" Violet asked with a grin.

"The secret's out," Henry said.

He stepped up to the booth and purchased two tickets. Then he and Violet were on their way to the elevators that were reserved for trips to the observation decks.

A uniformed man took their tickets and they were ushered into an elevator with the couple and their kids, who were speaking excitedly in a language Henry thought was German. Unlike the elevator that had taken them to the building's office space, this elevator had an attendant. The uniformed man waited to make sure no one else was coming, then pressed a button on the control panel.

The doors closed and Henry felt the bottom of his

stomach drop as they rose swiftly into the air. When he looked down at Violet, she was smiling ear to ear.

They emerged into a stylish vestibule, a silver sunbeam splayed across a ceiling painted deep purple. The family who had accompanied them on the elevator passed them, the mother seeming to issue instructions to the kids as they followed the signs marking the way to the observation deck. It made him think of his own mom, and he paused to pull his phone from his pocket.

"Give me one sec," Henry said to Violet.

He typed out a quick message to his mom.

THE ANTIQUES DEALER'S IN A MEETING. TAKING VIOLET TO TOP OF ESB WHILE WE WAIT.

He might be pushing his luck, but he had a feeling his mom would understand.

KEEP ME POSTED, KID.

He breathed a sigh of relief.

"Everything okay?" Violet asked.

"Everything's good," Henry said, pocketing his phone. He held out his arm. "My lady, your city awaits."

Thirty-Five

Violet's heart was full as Henry led her out the doors to the observation deck at the top of the Empire State Building, full of excitement and sadness and hope and loss all at once. It made her heart hurt, all that emotion spilling out of it.

It was late morning, the sun casting golden light on the water far below. The city was spread out beneath them, the skyscrapers rising like modern sculptures on all sides. She could see the shape of the city more clearly as they walked around the concrete deck, and she marveled at the way it seemed to come to a point at one end. She realized a moment later that the point was Battery Park, the very place she and Henry had started their journey.

"Look!" she said. "I think that's Battery Park!"

Henry put his hands on her shoulders. "I think you're right. Come on. I know a way we can be sure."

He headed for one of the clunky metal telescopes that dotted the observation deck. After digging in his pocket, he held out a handful of quarters to her.

"Take a look."

She took the quarters and followed the instructions on the telescope, then bent down to look through it. At first the view was blurry, and even more so when she tried to point it in the direction of Battery Park. Then everything clarified and she could see the Statue of Liberty lifting her torch over the water in the distance.

"It is!" she said. "It's Battery Park. I can see the Statue of Liberty. It looks so different from here. Everything looks different from here."

She watched as a small plane came into view over the water, towing some kind of banner behind it. She read its message silently as it passed in front of the telescope's view:

HAVE COURAGE AND BE KIND.

The plane drifted out of sight and she stepped back. "Take a look, Henry."

He bent down to look. "Everything's so much smaller." Then he straightened. "I think our time's up on the telescope. Everything went gray."

"Let's walk back to the other side where we can get a better view of the water," Violet said.

The observation deck was strangely quiet. They passed the German family, the three kids looking through telescopes like the one Henry and Violet had used to see the Statue of Liberty. Otherwise, there were only two other couples and a group of girls who didn't look much older than them.

"I think this as close as we can get to the water from up here," Henry said.

Violet looked past the gray and brown buildings and the grid of city streets to the wide band of blue shimmering below. The water meandered under a bridge, then curved out of sight. She had the sudden urge to follow it, to see where it led.

And it wasn't just the water. The desire to explore had been building in her since they'd arrived the day before. It had swept in on the wind that blew off the water on the way past the Statue of Liberty. She'd felt it in the hot breeze from the trains moving under the city, transporting people to and from places Violet could only imagine. Most of all, she'd sensed it in her own urge to break free—from her small life in Storybrooke, and even from Henry.

She immediately felt traitorous. Henry had made everything easier, paving the way so she didn't have to feel any fear or discomfort. She could hardly be angry. He loved her. Making things easier is what you do for the people you love.

This was her fault. She'd allowed it to happen, had willingly handed over all her decisions to Henry, to her teachers, to her father. It had started small: what kind of pizza to order, which subject to choose for an important essay, which electives to take at school.

But all those small decisions had turned into bigger ones. Now she couldn't remember the last time she'd made an important decision on her own—or even a small one, for that matter.

Actually, she knew exactly the last time she'd made a decision on her own; it had been the day before, when she'd insisted on listening to the man on the sidewalk outside Back in the Day. She'd made a decision again when she'd decided to look for Whitney Day at Tiffany and when she'd pressed Mildred for the name of Basil Knaggs.

All of those decisions had turned out fine. Most important, it had felt good to make them. She had felt strong and capable, like she could do anything.

She looked out over the city and was struck with the certainty that it was true. She could do anything—and maybe, just maybe, she was ready to do it on her own.

Thirty-Six

Henry looked out over the city, letting his eyes sweep across the water shining in the morning sun, the brick and steel and glass of the surrounding buildings, the cars crawling like ants below.

The view should have inspired him, but he could only feel defeated, his earlier enthusiasm for the observation deck tempered by Violet's silence and the feeling that they were somehow experiencing the whole thing separately.

It was easier to ignore the shift between them when they were moving through the city, when they were

busy dodging other pedestrians and figuring out subway schedules and trying to get the notebook. Then he
could tell himself the distance between them was just
stress or frustration—that everything would return to
normal when they got back to Storybrooke.

But here they were at one of the most romantic loca-
tions in the city, and Violet felt a million miles away. Just
a few weeks ago they would have held hands, snapped a
picture to post online, taken advantage of the opportunity to kiss without worrying about someone reporting
back to Violet's father. Now Violet stood in her own
space, an invisible wall between them as if she'd already
made the decision to leave, as if she were already moving
away from him.

He thought about his conversation with his mom on
the dinner cruise. He'd meant what he'd said about wanting Violet to be happy, so why was he fighting what was
beginning to feel like an inevitability? And why didn't
he mention it to Violet? Other than their brief dances
around the issue of their relationship, he'd avoided the

subject, telling himself the timing was all wrong, that the priority was to get the notebook.

Now they were alone with time to spare, and the thought of bringing it up terrified him. It was stupid. It wasn't like Violet would be angry. They were capable of having a conversation without fighting.

No, that wasn't the problem.

The real problem was that he was afraid of what she'd say if he brought up the subject, afraid the sick feeling he'd been carrying in his stomach for the past two days was his instinct telling him something Violet would only confirm. Once he'd said it, it couldn't be unsaid. The course of their relationship would be on another trajectory and there would be nothing he could do to stop it.

Regina always told him to listen to the little voice in his head, but he never understood what he was supposed to do if there was more than one voice. What if one voice told him to hold on tight to Violet and the other one told him to let her go? Or what if one voice told him to bring up the subject now while they were alone and let it play out, and the other voice told him to keep trying to prove they belonged together? What if one voice told him he and Violet were meant to be together forever and the other one told him this was the end of the line for them?

"Is something wrong, Henry?"

He looked down, almost surprised to find Violet still standing next to him. For a minute there, he'd felt almost like she was already gone.

He hesitated. Now was his chance. He couldn't hide forever. Wouldn't it be better to know, however painful the truth?

He smiled. "Nothing's wrong," he said. "I'm just enjoying the view."

Her face lit up as she turned her eyes back to the city. "It's so beautiful."

"It definitely is," he said, swallowing the words that seemed lodged in his throat.

She shivered a little. "It is a bit cold up here though."

Henry slid his arms out of his jacket and draped it around Violet's shoulders. He let his hands linger just for a moment, trying to banish the feeling that his days of being so familiar with her were numbered.

"You're not cold?" she asked, turning to him with a smile.

He shook his head. "It feels good after all that running around the city yesterday."

"Thanks."

He nodded and let his eyes travel to the smudge that was the Statue of Liberty at the end of the island. Passing by it on the ferry had been one of the most magical moments of their time together in the city. There was no point ruining the memory with some big conversation about their relationship that might not even be necessary.

They still had a chance to get the notebook, which meant Henry still had the chance to be Violet's hero. Maybe then Violet would see how much he loved her. He heard his mother's voice in his head.

That's what love is, Henry. It's doing things for someone because you love them, even when it's hard. That includes letting go.

But he wasn't ready to let go. Not yet.

Thirty-Seven

Violet took a deep breath as they headed back down to the lobby. Her initial euphoria at being on top of the world had morphed into melancholy. She couldn't quite put her finger on it, but it had something to do with Henry. They were fine when they were busy or around other people, but there was a new awkwardness when they were silent and alone.

It had never been that way between them, even when they'd first met. They'd gotten along immediately, talking for hours about Nicodemus and her father and music and Henry's moms and anything else that came to mind.

Now they almost felt like strangers, their conversations stilted.

She knew it had to do with her own realization that she wanted something different—different from Storybrooke, and different from letting everyone else take charge of her life. It wasn't a realization she could ignore. She would have to talk to him, but she could only handle so much at once. She would deal with the notebook first, then find a time that made sense to talk to Henry.

They emerged in the lobby and got into the elevators that would take them back to Basil Knaggs's office. She felt like they'd been in the Empire State Building forever, like they'd become trapped inside a labyrinth searching for an elusive treasure and were finally turning the last corner.

They stepped into the hall on the fifty-second floor and made their way back to Basil Knaggs's office. The woman who sat at the front desk smiled when she looked up.

"You came back," she said. "I'm glad. I'll let Mr. Knaggs know you're here."

"Thank you," Violet said.

She and Henry stood while they waited, looking at a series of black-and-white photos of the city that hung on the walls of the lobby. It was like watching a time-lapse photograph, the city growing up around a series of fields and open spaces that were quickly replaced with stone and brick and steel, the pastures morphing into concrete and asphalt. She could almost imagine what it had been like when the city was gritty and new and coal dust filled the air. Then there would have been no Washington Square, no Central Park, no Tiffany, no limousines or taxicabs.

"Well, hello there," a man said behind them. Violet turned to see a surprisingly dapper middle-aged man studying them with curiosity. "I'm Basil Knaggs. Helen tells me you're interested in one of my pieces."

He spoke with a crisp British accent. His dark blue suit was notably tailored, his shoes fashionable and modern. His strange name didn't suit him at all.

"That's right," Violet said. "I'm sorry to show up so suddenly. We're only in the city for a few more hours."

"Then there's no time to waste," Basil said. "Follow me."

They followed him down a wide carpeted hallway into a modest office. A window offered a view of blue sky, and in the distance, someplace that might have been New Jersey.

"Please sit," Basil said, lowering himself into a chair behind a simple desk. "Now how can I help you?"

Violet hurried to answer. She could've waited and let Henry step in, but those days were over. "I'm looking for an antique notebook," she said. "It's inscribed with the owner's name: Hank Morgan."

She intentionally withheld Mildred Appleby's name. Mildred had done them a favor. There was no need to be indiscreet if it wasn't necessary to their mission.

Lines formed on the bridge of Basil's nose. "I did recently acquire a piece that meets that description," he said. "May I ask why you're interested in it?"

"I believe it belonged to an ancestor of mine," Violet said. "It would mean a lot to my father to have it."

Basil shook his head. "I'm afraid I can't help you."

Violet had to hand it to him; he seemed genuinely sorry.

"I have money," Violet said. "It's not much, but I'll give you all I have."

"We both have money," Henry said. He glanced at Violet. "Please, it's really important we get the notebook before we leave the city later today."

"I'm sorry," Basil said. "I don't think I made myself clear. I can't help you because the notebook is no longer in my possession."

Thirty-Eight

Henry could hardly believe his ears. It would have been funny if Violet hadn't looked so stricken. It was like some cosmic force was trying to keep them from getting the notebook. If they'd been in Fairy Tale Land he would have assumed some sort of dark magic or trickery was at play, but in the here and now there was no reasonable explanation for all the obstacles they'd encountered.

"Didn't you just buy it three days ago?" Henry asked.

Violet shot him a warning look and he wondered suddenly if he wasn't supposed to mention Mildred Appleby.

She hadn't said anything about keeping it a secret when she'd given them Basil Knaggs's business card.

Basil looked only medium surprised. "Indeed, I did," he said. "I purchased it for a private collector and put it in the mail."

"A private collector?" Violet said.

He nodded. "It happens more often than you might think. Collectors become interested in all sorts of things. They represent a large portion of my business, actually, hiring me to search for pieces to add to their collections."

"Why would someone want an old notebook?" Henry asked. "Besides us, I mean," he added when Violet glared at him.

Basil shrugged. "I don't ask questions of my buyers. Their collections aren't my business, although I'd say it was likely a collector of early-nineteenth-century ephemera."

Henry wanted to reach out and hug Violet. He could see how disappointed she was by the way her shoulders sagged, the way her mouth turned down at the corners.

"I don't suppose you'd be willing to give us the name

of the buyer?" Henry asked. It was a long shot—Basil Knaggs seemed to be more businesslike than Mildred Appleby—but he had to ask. He couldn't bear to see Violet's defeat, and he wasn't crazy about his own, either.

Basil offered a cool smile. "I'm afraid not. Collectors don't purchase for profit. Once a piece is sold to a private collector, it often doesn't reemerge on the market for many years."

"So that's it then," Violet said.

Basil's expression softened. "I'm quite sorry. I can see this meant a lot to you. If it's any consolation, it went for quite a lot of money."

"It's not," Violet said. "But thank you."

Henry stood. It was rare for Violet to be so blunt, so cynical. He needed to get her out of there.

"Thank you," he said, reaching out to shake Basil's hand. "We appreciate that you took the time to meet with us."

"Yes, thank you." Violet's eyes were still dazed, but she reached out to shake Basil's hand as well.

He picked up two cards from a small gold stand on

his desk and handed one to each of them. "Let me know if there's ever anything I can do for you."

They nodded and said their goodbyes, then followed Basil out into the hallway. On the way out the door, Henry lifted a hand in farewell to the receptionist, who had been so nice to them.

Violet waited for the door to close before she leaned against the wall in the hallway.

"That's it," she said. "It's over."

"I'm so sorry, Violet," he said.

He'd known he loved Violet for a long time, but he'd never been as sure as he was at that moment. It was in the way his heart hurt like it was being crushed in a vise, in the way he would have done anything, given anything, to take away the sadness in her eyes.

"Maybe we can do an internet search when we get home," Henry said. "Basil said it went to a collector. Maybe a private collector would be proud enough of something new that they might post it online, or—"

"You can't fix this, Henry," Violet said.

"I'm just saying," he continued, then he sighed. "I hate to see you so sad."

"It's normal to be sad sometimes," she said. "You can't protect me from everything all the time." She looked at him. "And I don't want you to, Henry."

"Sorry," he said, stung. "I'm only trying to help."

"I know that, and I appreciate it," she said. "I think . . . I think I just want to go now."

He nodded and started for the elevators, Violet's words echoing in his mind.

You can't protect me from everything all the time. And I don't want you to, Henry.

Thirty-Nine

Violet stood silently next to Henry as the elevator descended to the lobby. She knew she'd hurt his feelings, but she didn't have the energy to think about Henry's feelings at that moment. They'd lost the note-book once and for all. Now there was no way to banish the sadness in her father's eyes, and if Basil Knaggs was right, it would probably be a long time before the note-book surfaced again, if it ever resurfaced at all.

She thought about her father working in the kitchen before she'd left Storybrooke, his slow movements hint-ing at his melancholy. She saw him as he'd been in

Camelot: vital, strong, even funny sometimes. For the first time, she wondered if it had been a mistake to stay in Storybrooke. What would her life have been like if they'd stayed in Camelot? Would her father still have been enthusiastic and full of ideas?

It was a tempting view from behind rose-colored glasses, but when she thought about how her own life would be different, it was impossible to be sorry they'd stayed in Storybrooke. Camelot held no future for her beyond marriage or perhaps a job as a lady-in-waiting in the king's castle. This world had given her so much. It had given her independence and knowledge and friendship.

It had given her Henry.

Whatever happened between them next, she was grateful for him. Even more important, she'd gotten a glimpse of another life, a life of excitement and possibility. More than ever, it was a life she knew she wanted.

But wanting something new would come at a price. It was becoming more and more obvious that she couldn't hold on to the past if she wanted to step into the future.

They exited the elevator and made their way out the big glass doors at the front of the Empire State Building. She looked back, letting her gaze sweep all the way to the top.

She would have to leave behind her hope of finding the notebook. It was lost to her forever, and like all things that were lost, she would have to let it go in order to seek out the unseen treasures ahead.

"Is there anything I can do?" Henry asked beside her.

She looked over at him and took his hand. "No, but thank you for asking, and for being here."

"Of course," he said. "I'll always be here for you, Violet."

She couldn't help wondering if he would still feel that way when she finally spoke the words she'd been holding in all day. He would be sad—he might even be angry—but it wouldn't change anything. She felt the inevitability of it echo through her deepest self.

To move into her future, she would have to let go of Henry, too.

"Let's get to the coffee shop before my mom starts to lose her patience," Henry said.

They found Emma and Killian at the same table they'd all occupied the day before. Emma had three empty paper cups in front of her and was folding a napkin into something that resembled a bird while Killian looked through a newspaper.

"Well?" Emma said when she spotted them making their way to the table.

Henry shook his head. "It's already been sold."

Disappointment shaded Emma's face. "Oh, no . . ." She hugged Violet. "I'm so sorry."

"It's okay," Violet said. She was surprised to find that she meant it. It turned out letting go wasn't easy, but it came with a kind of freedom once you did.

Emma rested a hand on Henry's shoulder. "You okay, kid?"

Violet really looked at him for the first time since they'd left the Empire State Building. Disappointment was written all over his face. It had never occurred to her that Henry was as invested in getting the notebook as she was. She'd been so wrapped up in her own pain she hadn't even noticed his.

"This is not how the story was supposed to end," Henry said. "How did we get it so wrong?"

Emma seemed to think about the question. "I'm not sure, but I think I know someone who might."

Forty

Henry looked out the window of the cab as it made its way over the Brooklyn Bridge. He had no idea where they were going, but he welcomed the distraction. After two days of trying desperately to find Sir Morgan's notebook while simultaneously trying to save his relationship with Violet, it was a relief to let someone else take charge. His mom had slid into the cab first and Henry had been more than happy to take the seat next to Killian. Violet had inexplicably claimed the front seat next to the taxi driver. Henry hadn't even tried to pay attention when his mom gave the cab driver the address.

They'd been driving for a good fifteen minutes before Killian finally spoke softly to him.

"Tough break, mate."

Henry nodded, still looking out the window. The loss he felt in the pit of his stomach had nothing to do with the fact that the city was receding in the rearview mirror and everything to do with the fact that Violet was receding with it. She might have been just a few feet away in the front seat, but there was no doubt in his mind that his time with her was coming to an end.

He just didn't know why.

"Want to talk about it?" Killian asked.

Henry glanced at the partition separating the back seat from the front of the cab. Was the partition soundproof? He wasn't sure, but Violet's gaze was directed out the cab's windshield. He could only assume she couldn't hear them over the noise of the city and with the partition between them.

He glanced over Killian at his mom, but she was either pretending not to hear them or lost in her own thoughts.

"I don't really know what to say," Henry finally said. "To be honest, I'm not even sure what's going on."

"With Violet you mean?"

Henry nodded.

Killian sighed. "Women: a mystery for the ages."

Any other time, Henry would have laughed, but he could barely manage a smile. "Everything was fine when we got here yesterday," Henry said.

"Are you sure about that?" Killian asked.

Henry didn't have to think too long to find the answer. "I guess not, but it seemed fine."

Killian was quiet for a minute. "One of the most important things about being at sea is learning to read the weather," he finally said.

Henry looked at him in disbelief. Were they even having the same conversation? What was Killian talking about?

"What does the weather at sea have to do with Violet and me?"

Killian shrugged. "It's just an observation. It sounds

easy, but some of the fiercest storms can seem to come out of nowhere. 'Seem' being the operative word."

"I'm still lost," Henry admitted.

"There's nuance to reading the weather," Killian continued. "A blue sky doesn't always mean smooth sailing. It took me a while—and a few lunches lost over the side—to start looking at the clouds, feeling the wind."

"Are you saying my relationship with Violet is like a storm at sea?" Henry asked.

"I'm saying there are usually signs of bad weather before the storm hits."

"But what if you read it wrong?" Henry asked. "What if you read it wrong and the next thing you know you're being tossed around like one of those empty bottles people throw into the ocean with a message?"

"Nothing you can do about it," Killian said.

"That's it?" Henry said. "That's your big piece of advice?"

"Technically, I haven't given you the actual advice yet," Killian said. "I've been setting it up."

"Can we get to the advice part?" Henry asked.

"Right. It's like this." Killian leaned a little closer. "Learning to read the weather is helpful only inasmuch as it allows you to be prepared. Once the bad weather hits, there's nothing to do but batten down the hatches and ride it out with whatever you've got on hand."

"Ride it out?" Henry was beginning to wonder if Killian had had something else to drink besides coffee while he waited for Henry and Violet to finish at the Empire State Building.

Killian nodded. "Ride it out and see where it takes you. Sometimes storms can pull you miles off course."

"Exactly," Henry said. "That's how I feel right now. Off course."

Killian seemed to think about it. "Something funny about being off course; I've never actually regretted any of the places I've ended up. Take Storybrooke, for instance. Never in a million years would I have steered a course for such a quiet place, not to mention a maddening woman like your mother—no offense."

Henry ignored the last part. It was Killian's half of the comedy routine he shared with Emma. "And now?"

Killian put an arm around Henry's shoulders. "Now? Well, now, I can't imagine my life without the quiet place or the maddening woman, not to mention her rather dashing, witty son."

"So, this is a complicated way of saying that everything turns out okay in the end," Henry said.

"No, this is a *riveting* way of saying that everything turns out okay in the end." Killian's tone grew more serious. "And that to fully experience the adventures to come, you have to move on from the ones you've already had."

Forty-One

Violet stepped out of the taxi onto the streets of Brooklyn and waited while Emma paid the cab fare. She had no idea why they'd made the trip across the bridge, but Emma seemed to have something in mind and Violet was too drained to ask questions.

Now she looked around, taking in the street, so different from those in Manhattan. Absent were the constant flow of traffic, the honking of horns, and the rush of the subway underfoot. It was more like a neighborhood, with small apartment buildings and houses on either side of a road fractured with cracked asphalt.

"That might be the most I've ever paid in cab fare," Emma said.

"What is this place, Mom?" Henry asked.

Violet wondered if the defeat in his eyes mirrored her own. To say they hadn't had the best couple of days was an understatement, and she felt a fresh rush of gratitude that he'd been so willing to sacrifice what should have been a wonderful trip to the city to search for her father's notebook.

"Let's call it a little perspective," Emma said, heading for the door.

They walked up a narrow set of concrete steps toward the doors of a brick building that looked like a small apartment house. Emma headed for one of the white doors and raised her hand to knock.

"I called ahead," she said when the knock was met with silence.

She was raising her hand to try again when the door flew open.

A slender man with thinning dark hair stood in the doorway.

"Isaac Heller," Killian said. "You have got to be kidding."

Violet looked with interest at the man in the doorway. As the former Author of The Book, Isaac knew more about the history of Storybrooke and its residents than anyone. He had, after all, created much of it.

Which still didn't shed any light on the reason for their visit.

"Hello, Isaac," Emma said. "Thanks for seeing us on such short notice."

"Just so we're clear that this can't become a habit," Isaac said, opening the door wider.

"We're not expecting to become best friends, if that's what you're worried about," Emma said.

They stepped into a small living room. The scent of musty carpet pervaded the room, which opened to a small kitchen divided from the living room by a yellowing countertop.

"Please have a seat," Isaac said, gesturing to a plain worn sofa flanked by armchairs. "Can I get you anything?"

"No, thanks," Emma said. "But I would like to speak to you in private."

"Very well," Isaac said. "Follow me."

Emma turned to the rest of them. "Be right back."

She followed Isaac down a narrow hall. A moment later, a door closed at the back of the house.

"Anybody else creeped out by this place?" Killian asked.

"I don't know," Violet said, wanting to be kind. "I suppose it's . . . quaint."

"Quaint my a—" Killian said.

"Do either of you know why we're here?" Henry interrupted.

Violet realized he hadn't yet spoken to her. He looked as miserable as she felt, and she suddenly wished they were alone. It couldn't be comfortable for him to be in the house of the former Author, especially after everything that had happened during the course of their trip. She had no idea what Emma was thinking, but she wished she could ask Henry if he was okay without Killian listening in. It was like being back in Storybrooke all over again. She already missed the anonymity of the city.

"I have no idea," Killian said. "This is all your mom's mission—and you know how she is when she's on a mission."

"I'm sure it's fine," Violet said. "If your mom brought us here, there's bound to be a good reason."

She'd barely finished speaking the words when the door at the back of the house opened. Emma reentered the living room trailing Isaac.

"Henry," Isaac said, "let's have a chat, shall we?"

Henry looked at Emma.

"It's okay, kid," Emma said. "Trust me."

Henry hesitated, then wiped his palms on his jeans and rose to his feet.

"Come along," Isaac said, heading back down the hall.

Henry glanced briefly from Violet to his mother, then followed Isaac to the unseen room at the back of the house.

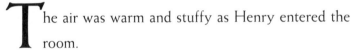

Forty-Two

The air was warm and stuffy as Henry entered the room.

"Close the door," Isaac said.

Henry followed his instructions, then looked around the room. It was the size of a small bedroom, with a narrow desk positioned against the wall under a window that overlooked a tiny yard overrun with weeds. The bookshelves on one wall practically groaned under the weight of the books lined up and stacked on every shelf. A cracked leather sofa, a tattered blanket thrown over one side, took up the length of another wall.

"Let's sit," Isaac said, gesturing to the sofa.

Henry sat nervously on the end of the sofa. He couldn't help being surprised that his mother had brought him to Isaac Heller's house, let alone that she was encouraging him to be alone with the former Author. Isaac hadn't exactly made things easy for the residents of Storybrooke.

"I'm not really sure why I'm here," Henry confessed when Isaac sat at the other end of the sofa.

Isaac studied him for a moment before speaking. "Your mother tells me you're having trouble with a story."

"I'm not working on The Book right now," Henry said. What had his mom been thinking?

Isaac's smile was cold. "I got the feeling it wasn't that kind of story."

Henry replayed his conversation with his mother in the coffee shop after he and Violet had found out the notebook was sold.

This is not how the story was supposed to end. How did we get it so wrong?

He stifled a sigh of frustration. How could his mom possibly think Isaac Heller could help him? His story with Violet was real and true. It wasn't something he could manipulate through The Book.

Henry stood. "I think my mom was confused. The story I'm struggling with is different from the rest of the ones in The Book."

He started for the door. He was sure his mom meant well, but this had been a mistake.

"Stories are more or less the same," Isaac said as Henry reached the door.

Henry turned around. "That's a dumb thing to say." He couldn't help himself. "You should know better than anyone that all stories are different. You've written them."

Isaac's expression didn't change. "Writing so many stories makes me uniquely qualified to make such a statement, wouldn't you say?"

"Normally," Henry said. He thought about all the stories in The Book, all the different things that had happened, all the unexpected twists and turns. "But it just doesn't make sense."

"You're thinking on a micro level," Isaac said. "You're concentrating on the details."

Henry returned to the sofa, intrigued in spite of himself. "What *should* I be concentrating on?"

"The big picture. The structure of all stories."

"The structure? Like the beginning, middle, and end?" Henry asked.

"For starters," Isaac said.

"For starters?" Henry shook his head. "Isn't the end, well, the end?"

Isaac seemed to consider the question. "It depends on how you look at it. What do you do after you finish reading a story—or writing one, for that matter?"

Henry still wasn't sure what Isaac was getting at. "I close it and put it back on the shelf? I put down my pen or close my computer?"

Isaac sighed. "Then what?"

"Then I . . . start another book, I guess? Start writing another story eventually."

"You guess or you know?" Isaac asked.

"I choose another book," Henry said with more certainty. "When I finish one book, I pick another one to read, and when I finish writing one, I start thinking about the next one."

"So, you might say the end of one story is in some ways the beginning of another?"

"I guess," Henry said, finally understanding Isaac's point. "But it's not like it's a continuation of the same story."

"Of course it is," Isaac said. "A character's exit doesn't mean he or she ceases to exist. As you know, they continue their story off the page."

He thought about the end of his and Violet's story. Violet would go on without him. She would attend college in some big, exciting city. She would make new friends and have new adventures.

The problem was that he didn't see his own future beyond their story as clearly.

"What if—as the author, I mean—you don't know what's next?" Henry asked.

Isaac smirked. "The best stories are those that are allowed to unfold in their own time, the stories that tell themselves through you, don't you agree?"

"What do we do in the meantime?" Henry asked.

"We listen," Isaac said. "We listen and we try to tell the story as it's meant to be told and not the way we want it to be told. We introduce those characters who seem to appear unbidden and we say goodbye to those whose time on the page has concluded."

"What if we're not ready to say goodbye?" Henry asked.

"That's irrelevant," Isaac said. "They must decide when it's time to go. It's only our job to listen."

The words fell like a stone in Henry's stomach. Isaac was right. There was no hanging on to Violet if she wanted to go. Deep down, he'd known that all along. He just hadn't wanted to admit it.

"I think I understand," he said, standing to leave. "Thank you. I know my mom told you to talk to me and . . . well, thanks."

He was almost to the door when Isaac spoke again.

"Henry?"

Henry turned to face him.

"There is an upside to saying goodbye to a compelling story," Isaac said.

"What's the upside?" Henry asked.

"We get a blank page to begin again."

Forty-Three

Violet stood on the patio at the back of Isaac's house, breathing in the fresh air. Well, not exactly fresh. It didn't have the bracing, briny scent of Storybrooke—more like exhaust and the smell of someone cooking bacon in a nearby house with the windows open—but it was better than the stale air of the house.

The living room had grown quiet after the departure of Henry and Isaac to the back of the house. Killian had immersed himself in an old issue of *Writer's Digest* from Isaac's coffee table while Emma paced the room. Violet had gotten the idea to get a breath of fresh air when she'd spotted a door off the kitchen leading to the patio.

She had no idea what they were doing there. The bus would leave for Storybrooke in three hours. It felt like an ending in more ways than one. The notebook was gone for good. She'd resigned herself to losing it.

It was harder to think about saying goodbye to Henry.

And she would have to say goodbye, at least to their romantic relationship. She thought about their time at the top of the Empire State Building, the strangely tense moment when she could have sworn they both knew how their trip to New York City would end.

Still, thinking it was one thing; saying it was something else.

The thought of hurting him was unbearable, but she owed herself something, too. She hadn't realized how imprisoned she'd felt by Storybrooke until she'd come to the city and had a taste of real freedom, and while Henry hadn't himself imprisoned her, she couldn't be the person she needed to be when she was with him. Their habits were too ingrained—Henry's need to protect and shelter her, Violet's willingness to let him do it because it was easier than thinking for herself.

Because it was easier than taking chances and being scared.

"Hey."

Henry's voice took her by surprise, and she turned to find him stepping out of the house and onto the patio.

"Hey," she said. "Is everything okay?"

He sighed. "Not really, but I think it will be."

She nodded, her throat closing around the sadness that threatened to spill over.

"Things aren't going to be the same when we get back home, are they?" Henry asked.

His voice was soft and even but the pain in his eyes was undeniable. She wanted to take it all back, all the things she'd learned about herself in the past two days, all the things she knew she wanted.

But that wasn't how it worked. You couldn't unknow yourself.

You couldn't unknow someone else, either.

She didn't want Henry to change for her—but she wasn't willing to change for him, either.

"I don't think so," she said softly, wanting to be both honest and kind.

He nodded. "Did I . . . Is it me?" he asked. "Did I do something wrong?"

"Of course not!" She crossed the patio and took one of his hands. "Please don't think that, Henry."

"Then what is it?" he asked.

"I'm not entirely sure." She forced herself to dig deeper. He deserved more. "Actually, that's not true. The truth is, I think maybe I've been a coward."

It was a relief to say it out loud. The thought had been reverberating through her mind since the day before, filling her with doubt and shame.

He looked genuinely confused. "What are you talking about, Violet? You're one of the bravest people I know."

"How can you say that? I don't do anything. I haven't done anything since I came to Storybrooke."

"Coming to Storybrooke was brave all by itself," he said. "It's like moving to another country times a hundred. You had to learn everything from scratch."

"I had you," she said sadly.

"I didn't figure it out for you, Violet," Henry said. "I tried to make it easier, but you did it. You learned how to drive a car and how to use a computer and how to talk like you didn't just step out of a Jane Austen novel."

Violet laughed a little even as tears stung her eyes.

He reached out to touch her cheek. "Asking for help doesn't mean you're not strong." He dropped his hand. "But I have a feeling there's more to it than that."

She exhaled a long shuddering breath. "Oh, Henry . . . I don't know where to begin."

Forty-Four

Henry knew it was over. It had been in the air almost since the moment they'd ditched the group on Ellis Island; he'd just been trying to ignore it, trying to turn back the clock or find some rhyme or reason in it.

Now there was no denying it. He saw it in her sad expression when she looked at him, like she was just trying to figure out how to say goodbye.

"Start at the beginning," he said. "Or as close to it as you can."

She drew in a breath and nodded. "I've figured out

that it's too easy to let things happen," she said. "You just let go, let the people around you make the decisions, accept whatever happens as a consequence of other people being in control. It's so much harder to make things happen, to make decisions even when they might steer you wrong or hurt you later—or even worse, hurt someone else."

Henry thought carefully about how to respond. There were lots of reasons he didn't want to beg Violet to stay, humiliation for one. After all, how pathetic did a guy have to be before he looked like a total loser?

But there was something more important than looking desperate: Violet. He loved her. He wanted her to be happy. Even if it was possible to keep her in Storybrooke—to keep her with him—it wouldn't be worth the price of her happiness.

"We all have to figure that stuff out," he said gently. "When to ask for help and when to stand on our own, when to take a chance and when to play it safe."

"But how am I supposed to learn to stand on my own

when there are so many people propping me up?" she asked. "I've been so lucky to have family and friends who love me, who are willing to do so much for me, but how do I become someone who can make decisions and take charge of my life if I don't actually try it?"

It was too hard to look into her eyes, to see how much she meant everything she was saying, how much it hurt her to say it. He looked out across the overgrown yard instead.

"Will you be able to do that in Storybrooke?" he asked.

It took her a moment to answer. "I don't think so. Being in Storybrooke makes it too easy to be Violet Morgan, damsel in distress."

He looked at her. "You have never been a damsel in distress."

"I think maybe I have, and that's okay. I just can't keep doing it. Next year we'll graduate from high school. I'm terrified, but you know what?"

"What?"

"It feels good."

"To be terrified?" he asked.

She smiled "Yes. To be terrified. To not know what's going to happen next. To not have all the answers and not rush to someone else to give them to me," she said. "I think maybe I need to be scared a little."

Henry didn't want to admit it, but he understood. He'd been playing it safe, too, letting his moms fix things for him when they got too weird, knowing Killian and his grandparents were there for backup, hiding in the sameness of Storybrooke and the people he'd known forever and the security of his relationship with Violet.

"If it makes you feel any better," he said, "I've relied at least as much on you."

"You have?"

He nodded. "You've been my best friend since the moment you came to Storybrooke. You've made it easy to be happy without even doing anything or going anywhere."

"Thanks?"

"You know what I mean." He looked in her eyes. "I'm just sorry I couldn't be your hero one last time."

She shook her head. "What are you talking about?"

"We didn't get the notebook," Henry said. "I can't help thinking we might have gotten our hands on it if I'd made better plans or insisted on calling Back in the Day last week."

"You've been my hero since the day I met you, but it's time to be my own hero now," Violet said. "And that means accepting responsibility when things don't work out the way I plan—or don't plan. I'm the one who owes you an apology."

Henry couldn't hide his surprise. "An apology? For what?"

"We ran all over the city for two days for nothing. We missed Ellis Island and the wax museum and bowling and the Met," she said.

"Yeah, but if we hadn't gone looking for the note-book we would have missed getting lost, meeting the poet outside Back in the Day, seeing Tiffany, meeting

Whitney Day and Mildred Appleby, and seeing the city from the top of the Empire State Building. Plus, think of all that homework we're going to catch up on while we're grounded."

She laughed.

"Seriously, though," he continued, "this has been the most exciting two days of my life. I'll remember it forever and there's no one I would rather have spent it with than you."

She looked into his eyes. "It was awesome, wasn't it?"

He knew she wasn't just talking about New York City. She was talking about them—about all the jokes and laughter and long talks and little arguments, all the French fries and school dances and stolen kisses and walks home from school.

Most of all, she was talking about the love that had blossomed between them when they were just two kids trying to figure out the world—and themselves.

"It was the best," he said. "I'll never forget it."

Not everything is meant to last forever.

"Will we still be friends?" he asked softly.

She leaned in and he wrapped his arms around her. "Always," she said against his shoulder. "Always."

She looked up at him and for a long moment there was nothing but her eyes and the beautiful face he knew so well. When he touched his lips to hers the rest of the world melted away, just like always. He closed his eyes and tried to memorize the feel of her in his arms, the soft press of her lips against his.

When they pulled apart, tears shone at the corners of her eyes. Henry blinked back his own.

A soft chirping from Violet's bag interrupted the moment and Violet reached into it for her phone.

"It's from my father," she said, unlocking the screen. "I hope someone hasn't told him we ran off. That will definitely be better coming from . . ."

Her face turned a shade paler. He was about to ask her if she was all right when she started laughing.

"Violet . . ." She just kept laughing, tears rolling down her cheeks until he started to worry she was losing it. "You're scaring me, Violet."

"It's my . . . father," she gasped. "He . . . he bought it!"

She turned the phone around to show Henry the picture on the screen. It was the notebook he and Violet had been hunting since the moment they'd landed in New York City—the one they had thought they'd lost.

Catching her breath, she turned the phone around to read the text from her father. "He says he bought it from an antiques dealer in New York."

"Want to place bets on whether the dealer's name was Basil Knaggs?" Henry asked.

Violet looked up from the phone. Now Henry was laughing.

"I can't believe it," Violet said. "We covered almost the entire city trying to get the notebook, and the whole time we were competing against my father."

"Just another thing to add to all the other crazy things that have happened since we've been here," Henry said.

She smiled up at him. "Anything else you'd like to add to the list before we go back to Storybrooke?"

"I don't think I can handle any more crazy, but there is something I'd like to do," he said.

She smiled and took his hand. "Whatever it is, I'm in."

Forty-Five

Violet stepped into the carriage at the edge of Central Park and sat down while Henry climbed in after her. Up ahead, the carriage carrying Emma and Killian was already in motion.

The driver glanced back to make sure Henry and Violet were settled, then flicked the reins over the majestic white stallion at the front of the carriage. They moved forward with a jolt and Violet grabbed on to the side as the wheels started moving. A few seconds later, the carriage settled into a smooth rhythm.

She relaxed and looked up, the endless blue sky stretching above the partial roof of the carriage, the skyscrapers surrounding the park visible above the tops of the trees. After days of worry, it was liberating to let go of the search for her father's notebook, especially since she knew he'd gotten it anyway. She'd felt his excitement even in the text he'd sent her. Maybe the notebook would remind him of who he was by inspiring him to create again.

She'd already decided to apply to colleges in New York City, Boston, and Chicago, maybe even Seattle. She would cast her wishes into the fountain of life and trust that the right ones would come true. She had a feeling her father would be just fine. If he needed her, she would only be a plane or bus ride away. In the meantime, she was ready to think about herself for a change.

She inhaled the scent of freshly cut grass, all the tension she hadn't even been aware of leaving her body once and for all.

"Do you like it?" Henry asked.

She looked over at him with a grin. "It's amazing, Henry. Thank you."

He wrapped his arm around her as she leaned her head against his shoulder. She inhaled the scent of him, trying to engrave the moment on her mind, the feeling of well-being she had in his arms and the knowledge that she'd always been safe and loved with him.

They had come so far together. They'd been children when they'd become friends, had grown into young adults together. They'd shared their first kiss, had learned what it meant to really love someone, to sacrifice and compromise for them.

Nothing would ever change those things, but now it was time for something new.

An achingly beautiful and familiar melody carried across the afternoon air, a man in a black hat stretching a bow across the strings of a violin as they passed. The strains of "Somewhere Over the Rainbow" followed their carriage like a blessing.

Violet sat up and Henry's arm fell away. She kissed his cheek and let her eyes travel outside the carriage, across the people walking the meandering paths through the park, over the rolling green lawns and groupings of trees that hid everything beyond them from view. The rest of the world was out there somewhere.

And a new fairy tale was waiting.